NURSE IN A CORNER...

As his eyes slid over her, they were filled with a naked, brutal hunger that made Laura feel panic. This man would not be easy; she would have her hands full with him.

She met his stare, smiling, her eyes warm and limpid and filled with a provocative promise that tensed the man's nerves to a screaming need. But he could wait, and it would be worth waiting for. He nodded at last and turned away.

"I'll make the arrangements and let you know," he said.

Laura felt a momentary weakness. A mistake would be more than she could afford now.

"You are going to help me?" she stammered and her voice sounded incredulous.

Phil turned.

"Sure—I'm going to help you—and then you're going to be mine—for as long as I want you. Is that clear?"

doctor
PRESCOTT'S
secret

PEGGY GADDIS

WILDSIDE PRESS

PART ONE

1. Office Nurse

Dr. STEVEN PRESCOTT LET HIM-self quietly into his private office by a side entrance. He listened for a moment to the low buzzing sound coming from his reception room beyond the door with its glazed white panel. The room was full, the sound told him. But of course it would be, today being his clinic day for charity cases.

He hung up his hat and coat, donned the white jacket which was the badge of his profession, and seated himself wearily behind his desk. The night had taken a lot out of him. He wanted nothing more in the world than to crawl into a snug, warm bed and sleep at least twelve hours. The very thought twisted his mouth with a wry, humorless grin. Imagine any doctor nowadays getting more than a few hours of sleep!

He looked up sharply as the door into the reception room opened and closed behind a woman in the white uniform of a nurse. She was lovely, and carried her shining blonde head with an assurance that said she was quite aware of her loveliness. Through the thin stuff of her uniform, that moulded itself to her beautiful curves, her skin was rose-petal tinted and looked smooth and soft—Dr. Prescott wrenched his mind away from that direction, remotely startled that he should have had such thoughts in the first place. Of course, she was still new here. Maybe that explained it.

"Good morning, Doctor," said the nurse pleasantly, and there was the tiniest possible smile complete with a dimple at one corner of her lovely mouth, as though she were quite aware of his thoughts and relished them.

"Doctor, you're worn out," she said softly, almost tenderly.

7

"A pretty rugged night," he admitted. "The hospital called me at two . . . Doris Blake—I—lost her."

"Oh, I'm so sorry," the warm melody of her voice slid soothingly along his jangled nerves. "And—the baby?"

A faintly wry look touched Steve's clean-cut, generous mouth.

"Seven-and-a-half pounds and yelling its head off in the nursery this very moment, I have no doubt," he said grimly. "I hope I'll never have another job as tough as breaking such news to the husband."

"But, Doctor, I looked at her case history," said Laura quickly. "You warned them two years ago, when their second child was born, that it would be dangerous for them to attempt another child."

Steve nodded. "People just won't listen, Miss Weston."

There was a small silence. Then Laura Weston, moving away to a stand beside the window covered with a fresh white towel, said over her shoulder, "I suppose the husband will have to allow somebody to adopt the kids?"

Steve stared at her, unpleasantly startled by the suggestion.

"Not as long as he draws breath," he said sharply. "I know him. He'll manage somehow—his mother will help. No, there's no danger that Jerry will allow the children to be adopted—"

Laura came back, bearing a steaming cup of coffee which she had poured from a thermos jug on the towel-covered stand.

Steve drank the coffee gratefully and smiled his thanks at her. And then Laura moved around behind his chair, her gray-green eyes warmly compassionate. She drew his head back to her breast and passed cool, deft fingers across his aching head.

Her manner was so casual, so matter of fact—almost, Steve had the crazy thought, the way Susie, his wife, would have comforted Junior or Bill for a bumped head, that for a moment he relaxed against her and felt the warm, vibrant firmness of her bosom like a scented pillow beneath his aching head. The tight bands of pain began to relax and he made no protest against her deft, soothing touch.

"Unfasten your collar, Doctor," she said crisply after a moment, her tone completely impersonal, the tone of any nurse to any patient. And in spite of himself, Steve found himself obeying her, loosening his tie, unbuttoning his collar.

Laura's cool fingers slipped down inside his collar at the back of his neck and began to massage with gentle, upward strokes along the back of his neck and across his shoulders, her fingers cool and smooth against his bare skin.

Steve was still for a moment, accepting her ministrations gratefully, but at last he stirred and looked up, surprising for an instant an unexpected warmth in her gray-green eyes, an expression gone almost before he could be quite sure that it had been there.

Instantly she was once more—if she had ever been anything else—the coolly impersonal, smartly efficient nurse.

"Is that better, Doctor?" she asked pleasantly.

Fastening his collar, getting his tie straight, Steve said quite honestly, "That's wonderful! I feel as if I'd had an hour's nap. You're quite a person. I still wonder at my luck in finding an office nurse like you."

Laura's laugh was light and warm, and there was a twinkle in her eyes.

"You didn't find me, Doctor," she told him daringly. "I found you. I've wanted to work for you for more than a year. I used to watch you at the hospital. I've seen you operate. I know how much good you do among the poor and that you never refuse a call, even when you know the patient can't pay you. You see, Doctor, I know quite a lot about you, even if I've only been working for you a week. So when I found your nurse was leaving to be married, I raced right over before anybody else could beat me to the job."

No man could fail to be flattered and Steve grinned at her.

"I think if I'd already hired somebody else, I'd probably have fired her when you showed up," he admitted frankly.

"Why—thank you, Doctor," she said softly, smiling at

him warmly, before she lowered her eyelids demurely. "I'm—very happy that you feel that way."

For a moment, perhaps for no reason whatever except that the back of his neck seemed still to tingle from the touch of her cool, deft hands, Steve was disturbed, oddly and foolishly. But the next instant he was himself again.

"Well, shall we get on with the morning's work?" he suggested, and because he was puzzled and faintly uneasy because of that stirring in his blood at the touch of her fingers on his naked skin, his voice was almost curt.

Laura studied him for just an instant, a faint flicker of amusement in her eyes as though she were completely aware of his disturbance and its cause. Then she spoke a colorless affirmative and admitted the first of the waiting patients.

It turned out to be a day that differed not one whit from his usual routine, except for those brief moments when she had so deftly dispelled his headache. And by the time he had finished that day, and said good night to her, he did so without a second glance, and so missed the slight tightening of her wantonly lovely mouth and the chill flash that lit her eyes.

As he turned in at the drive that led to the garage set back from his home he slowed as he always did and let his eyes absorb the scene before him. The low white ranch-type house glowed with lights in every window, that seemed to laugh at the chill November night. Through looped-back, extravagantly ruffled white organdy curtains, he could see Susie in the dining room, putting the finishing touches to the table. His heart warmed with loving tenderness.

As the car rolled into the garage, the door from the kitchen burst open and two small, tow-headed boys raced out and flung themselves upon him, babbling their joy at his return. Steve bent, laughing, tucked a delighted small boy beneath each arm and went up the walk and into the house. There he set down the boys and steadied himself automatically for Susie's inevitable wild rush into his arms.

"Golly, did I miss you!" She crowded closer in his arms,

and took the lobes of his ears in her two hands and stood on tiptoe so she could reach up to kiss him, with the warm, unashamed passion that seven years of marrige had never dulled. A fact Steve knew to be pretty wonderful and for which he never ceased to be deeply grateful. It made living with Susie a constantly exciting, stimulating delight. She never failed to greet him as though they had been separated for weeks—though as a matter of fact they had spent only four nights apart in the seven years of their marriage, and that had been when her father had died.

The boys on either side of them clamored for attention. Susie, without the slightest intention of loosening her grip on Steve, spoke over her shoulder to them. "Scat, you two! Can't you see we're busy? Go 'way somewhere—quick!"

Steve laughed in delight, kissed her and put her a little away.

"Woman, have you no maternal feelings for your young?" he asked sternly.

"Sure, scads of them, only they don't seem to be uppermost at the moment," she admitted. "Why is that, do you suppose? Do you think maybe I have my mind on—other things?"

Her tone was innocent, her eyes were wide but there was a mocking imp dancing at the back of their brown-gold depths as he kissed her again.

"I hope so," he told her very softly, in a tone that brought a tide of happy color to her cheeks. "I hope so, indeed."

From the kitchen doorway a mellow voice now touched with a tinge of long-suffering patience said, "If you two done lovin' each other, dinner's ready."

"We'll never be done loving each other," said Susie firmly.

Above her brown head Steve grinned at the buxom Negro woman in the kitchen doorway, and her face split with a wide white-toothed smile that was warm with liking.

"Hi, Minnie," he greeted her.

"Hi, Doctor," said Minnie and added sternly, "You have your lunch today?"

"I'm not sure, Minnie—I guess not, though, for I'm starved—" said Steve frankly.

Instantly Susie's laughter vanished and she drew him anxiously towards the dining room, settling him almost as she would the two boys.

"I'll bet that snooty new nurse of yours forgot to remind you to eat—I hate that creature. She's so—" in time Susie remembered the two boys and spelled it out carefully, "—d-a-m-n-e-d beautiful."

"Well, after all, it's not one of her duties to see that I eat—" Steve defended Laura, and once more felt the cool tingling sensation of her hands across the back of his neck and his forehead.

"I suppose not," Susie was being merely polite about it and not at all convinced.

She studied him unobtrusively while they finished dinner and when she had put the boys to bed and came back to the living room, to find him reading the evening paper. She paused beside him, cocked her head inquiringly and Steve grinned, throwing the paper aside and welcomed her into his lap, where she curled as contentedly as a kitten, her head against his shoulder.

"I don't suppose you'd consider letting me disconnect the telephone," she suggested tentatively, and even before he answered, she sighed. "Of course not. Golly, I should know by now that you're too much like Dad to refuse to crawl out of a warm bed at three in the morning to drive miles in a blizzard to treat somebody's cut finger or earache."

Steve kissed the tip of her impertinent, slightly tip-tilted nose.

"I take that reference to your father as a very sincere compliment," he told her fondly.

"Well, you better had, because he was quite a lad, my Dad," said Susie firmly. "But then, you're quite a lad, too."

Suddenly as she clung to him, her gaiety fled, and she burrowed her face against his shoulder, clinging to him almost frantically.

"I'm—scared," she whispered in a small shaken voice.

"Scared? Why, darling?" asked Steve, holding her close.

"Because we're so happy. Because I love you so much. Because something—awful might happen to us. I'd die if anything happened to you—" her voice came in a small, strangled wail.

And even as his arms tightened about her and his lips found her own and he soothed her momentary but very real terror, he had the most absurdly vivid memory of cool, smooth fingers moving deftly across his aching forehead and the taut muscles at the back of his neck and along his shoulders.

Almost as though such a memory might be an insult to Susie, he lifted one of her small, grubby paws, roughened with housework and her beloved gardening, the inexpertly applied nail-polish chipped and broken, and touched it to his lips. Susie looked up, flushed, shy, winking very fast to control the tears that glistened in her eyes that brimmed with her adoration of him.

"Let's—go to bed, darling," she whispered against his ear. "Before that damned telephone starts ringing its head off."

And laughing softly, he lifted her to her feet and they went up the stairs, his arm about her.

2. Fair Warning

MRS. JOHN LOGAN WAS STEVE'S richest—and most troublesome, he sometimes thought—patient. She occupied an apartment at the Cheswick Towers, the city's newest and most luxurious apartment-hotel. A vast block-long square, built around an expensive and painstakingly cared for patio.

Steve was making his weekly call on her a few evenings later when, crossing the lobby, he came face to face with Laura. She wore a smartly tailored tweed suit and a mink shoulder-cape swung from her shoulders.

"Why, Doctor," she greeted him with pretty surprise, "what in the world are you doing here?"

"Making a routine call on a patient, Mrs. Logan," he told her, puzzled, admiring her expensive beauty but wondering. "And now, what are you doing here?"

"Oh, I live here," she told him gaily and added teasingly, "Don't look so surprised, Doctor. I have a small income in addition to my salary—and I like being comfortable."

"Who doesn't?" Steve agreed as they walked towards the bank of elevators.

"Have you had dinner, Doctor?" she demanded as they waited for the elevator.

"No time," he admitted ruefully. "I'll pick up something on the way to the hospital—"

"Oh, but that's not good for you, Doctor," she protested eagerly. "Look, why don't you stop by my place after you've paid your call and share a steak with me? I hate eating alone yet I have to do such a lot of it—and it's really quite a noble steak! Much too big for one person."

The elevator door slid open and he followed her into it, formulating excuses, but even before he could put them

14

into words, she had laid her gloved hand on his in a small, fleeting gesture that was very coaxing.

"After all, why not? You have to eat and I have quite a way with a steak, if I must say it myself—and it will save time for you." As the elevator door slid open for her, she laughed over her shoulder at him and said gaily, "The steak will be ready when you are."

Steve blinked, not yet having had a chance to offer any protest. As the elevator let him off at the next floor, he shrugged wearily and put thoughts of Laura out of his mind.

Old Mrs. Logan was waiting for him, along with her equally old and harassed-looking maid, who constantly indicated that living with Mrs. Logan was a burden scarcely to be borne. Yet Steve knew the two elderly women were devoted to each other. Mrs. Logan was a chronic arthritis case, and in almost constant pain. Very little could be done for her, though Steve did all that was humanly possible. He had guessed some time before that Mrs. Logan got quite a kick out of his weekly visits, and their mock-insulting repartee; if it amused her to abuse him with her wicked little tongue, surely the poor old soul was entitled to that much pleasure.

When he had done what he could for her, he hesitated only a moment at the elevator and then walked back to the service stairs and down one flight to the apartment door that bore a card reading *Miss Laura Weston.* He stood there for a moment, frowning, before at last he lifted his hand to the bell and pushed the button.

There was a brief delay and then the door opened and Laura stood there smiling at him, flushed as she zipped her powder-blue housecoat up to its low collar beneath her pretty chin.

"Do come in," she invited hospitably. "I was just getting into something dry. It's such a beast of a night outside."

She ushered him in to a living room that was large and tastefully decorated. Warm with the light of several artfully shaded lamps, bright with hand-blocked linen draperies and blond furniture. An open fire glowed, adding its final touch of comfort and cheer, beneath a low white mantel on which there was a low bowl of rich red roses.

She indicated a comfortable chair beneath a reading lamp, with the evening paper laid on the wide arm. She brought him a cocktail, the delicate thin glass faintly frosty.

"Do make yourself comfortable," she begged prettily. "Dinner will be ready in a jiffy—or at least, a jiffy-and-a-half."

With a whisper of her silken skirts she went away into the tiny, gleaming kitchenette and Steve relaxed then in the comforting atmosphere. Realizing for the first time how tired and hungry he was, he sniffed appreciatively at the fragrant smell of broiling steak.

Dinner was served on a gate-leg table near the fire. Yellow pottery dishes splashed with vivid flowers on a crisp linen cloth; yellow candles in black glass holders. The steaks lived up to everything she had claimed for them; the salad was crisp and delectable; the broccoli had a tangy cream-and-cheese dressing; and the hot apple pie served with a large thin slice of yellow cheese melted in his mouth.

Over coffee and cigarettes, he studied her curiously.

"You're really an amazing woman," he admitted frankly.

She smiled, her lovely brows arched.

"In a nice way, I do hope, Doctor?" her tone was gaily mocking.

"Oh, in a thoroughly nice way," he assured her, his tone matching hers. "I mean it hasn't been thirty minutes since I came in here, yet you have just served a delicious meal that should have taken hours to prepare."

She tilted back her lovely head, the crisp shining curls catching and imprisoning the light from the yellow candles, and laughed.

"Oh, Doctor!" she mocked. "How long does it take to pop frozen vegetables into a pressure cooker, broil a couple of steaks and slip a frozen pie into the oven? Any woman who isn't a good cook nowadays is one who can't read, surely. All you have to do is follow the printed directions on the package."

"Do tell!" he marveled lightly. "And here for years I've been hearing about what a hard lot in life women have. Slaving over a hot stove all day, doing the week's wash, scrubbing, cleaning—"

"Pure propaganda, Doctor," she assured him. "Of course, I'm a traitor to my sex when I confess it, but all that is just to make the poor deluded male feel 'the little woman' deserves sympathy—and, maybe, a larger house-keeping allowance."

It was very pleasant here in this bright, warm im-maculately kept room. Laura, her shining hair in exquisite order, the satin housecoat moulding itself to every exquisite curve of her alluring body, was an enchanting dinner com-panion. But suddenly Steve had an odd sense of urgency and stood up.

"Much as I hate to do it, I have to get going," he told her firmly.

Without protest she was on her feet, bringing his coat, holding it for him, handing him his hat even as she spoke.

"I know. I hate your having to go but I know you must, because you have a consultation at the hospital with Dr. Hurst at eight-thirty and he'd never forgive you if you kept him waiting even a moment. He's such a—stuffed shirt," and for the first time there was an edge of anger in her voice.

"Why, nurse!" he protested, a little startled yet making his voice light and teasing. "A nurse, daring to speak so of a doctor! That's almost blasphemy—it simply isn't done!"

Laura's laugh was taut.

"That's what you think," she mocked. "Just as well you can't be present when nurses get together, off duty, out of reach of listening ears and the subject of doctors comes up—as it always does. It would set you back on your heels!"

"I'm glad I can't overhear them," Steve grinned. "I'm afraid it would destroy my self-confidence completely."

"Oh, you have nothing to worry about," she told him and all pretense of raillery was gone from her voice, and he knew that she was suddenly completely in earnest.

"You are the one doctor in a thousand for whom any nurse would sell her soul."

"Oh, come now—" protested Steve, annoyed with himself for the momentary feeling of embarrassment and confusion that came over him.

Laura smiled warmly, understanding his emotion completely.

"I'm sorry if I embarrass you, Doctor, but it's quite true. I hadn't meant to blurt it out like this," she lowered her eyes as though unwilling for him to see whatever secret they held. "It's just that—well, we all admire you so much at the hospital. My goodness, why do you think I gave up a good salary, plus expenses, for an eight-hour shift on private duty?"

Steve hesitated and then said awkwardly, "I admit that's puzzled me. It's very good of you and I appreciate the compliment enormously. But I hardly feel it's right to allow a nurse of your ability to work for the much smaller salary I am able to pay—"

Laura brushed that aside with a hand that was white and smooth, each nail a shining, perfect oval delicately rose-colored.

"The salary is not nearly as important as being associated with a person I admire and respect," she assured him quietly. "And I told you I have a small private income that pays for all this. And you're really going places, Dr. Prescott. I'll learn a great deal, working for you, that will make me a better nurse. And as your practice grows, you will be able to pay me better, and I'll have the satisfaction of knowing that I'm—well, almost a partner, not just an employee. Don't you think that a doctor and a nurse who work together smoothly and efficiently, as you and I do, is a pretty wonderful thing? It's—well, a compensation far more important to me than mere money. After all, Dr. Prescott, I want some day to be as good a nurse as you are a doctor. That's worth a great deal to me."

"Thanks. That's about as nice a tribute as any man could ever hope for," he told her sincerely. "Thanks for a wonderful dinner, too, and the relaxing hour. I'll go out now and hold my own with Hurst—stuffed shirt or not."

"Of course you will. And thanks for dining with me. It's been a lot of fun. I do hope we can do it again—very soon," she told him warmly, and closed the door behind him, listening to his footfalls as he went down the corridor.

She leaned her back against the closed door and stood there for a moment, her eyes narrowed, her mouth a thin, almost ugly line of cynical amusement.

"The poor damned fool!" she said softly, speaking barely above her breath. "It's going to be easy. Almost too easy. Like taking candy from a sick baby! And—I think it's going to be—fun, too!"

And Dr. Prescott would have been seriously puzzled, perhaps justifiably uneasy, if he could have heard her laughter there alone in the bright warm room.

But Dr. Prescott was hurrying to the vast block-square hospital, eyeing his watch uneasily as he parked the car. He saw that despite his haste he was going to be five minutes late for his consultation.

Dr. Hurst brusquely accepted his apologies. When the consultation was over, and he was preparing to leave the hospital, Dr. Hurst detained him for a moment, the plump, well-fed face which topped his short, rotund figure holding a slight frown.

"By the way, Prescott—" He hesitated.

Steve waited politely.

"Probably unpardonable of me, but I feel I should offer you—shall I say, a word of warning," said Dr. Hurst and managed an awkward smile. "Though you are not a boy, I'm quite a bit older than you and . . . I do assure you that I have your interests at heart."

"That's very kind of you, Dr. Hurst."

"Not at all—not at all," Dr. Hurst brushed that aside. "I—er—understand you have a new office nurse?"

"Yes, I have. Miss Graham left to get married."

"This new nurse, Laura Weston—you find her—capable?"

"Very much so."

"Er—well, yes—no one has found any fault with

her—er, efficiency—her skill as a nurse. I'm afraid it's Laura Weston as a woman against whom I should—er—warn you," said Hurst, and to Steve's astonishment he saw small beads of perspiration on the plump, ruddy face.

"I'm afraid I'll have to ask you to explain that, Doctor," said Steve coldly.

"Er—well, naturally." Dr. Hurst was uncomfortable but determined. "I suppose you know that she was fired from the hospital for—er—insubordination?"

"I didn't—she came to me from private duty work."

"Yes, of course," said Dr. Hurst and there was a mean look in his pale blue eyes. "You remember Dr. Anna Harmon?"

Steve looked startled.

"You mean the Senior Interne who was making such a fine record and who suddenly went off the deep end—narcotics, wasn't it? And bungled her work so badly a patient died?"

"That's the one," said Dr. Hurst and his eyes were cold, his mouth grim. "She was in obstetrics—doing a fine job—until she came on duty heavily under the influence of liquor and before any one could stop her—" he made a gesture of dismissal. He added grimly, "Fortunately for the hospital, the woman was a charity patient—which doesn't make Dr. Harmon's crime any the less despicable, but it did—er—relieve the hospital of pressure that might have been—well, most unfortunate."

"I remember, of course," said Steve, frowning. "But may I ask what all this has to do with my office nurse?"

"She and Harmon were pals—very chummy—I understand they still are—"

Steve had difficulty controlling his anger, and his tone was biting, despite his efforts, when he said, "Then you are condemning Nurse Weston merely because she is loyal to her friends?"

Dr. Hurst flushed beneath the tone and his eyes were cold.

"Nothing of the kind," he said harshly. "I merely felt you should be warned of your nurse's—er—refusal to obey instructions, which was what brought about her dismissal —not her friendship with Harmon."

"Thanks, Doctor," said Steve harshly. "I'll—bear it in mind."

Dr. Hurst looked after him, his face sour with anger as Steve, unwilling to trust himself any further, turned and strode out into the night, lashed now with sleet, and a bitter wind.

3. Baby for Sale

STEVE HAD WONDERED JUST WHAT Laura's manner would be next morning, after that hour of something closely approaching intimacy. But when he reached his office Laura greeted him exactly as she had greeted him the day before.

Gradually as the days passed and she did not by so much as a word or gesture attempt to recall anything of that blissfully relaxing hour he had spent in her apartment, he stopped thinking about it. Stopped thinking about that first morning she had put aside her impersonal manner and had massaged away his headache; he thought only fleetingly of the bright, luxurious apartment where everything had gleamed with order and comfort and good cheer.

There came an evening perhaps a week or more after the dinner, when he was alone in the living room finishing a painstaking perusal of the current month's medical journal, when the telephone rang imperiously. Swiftly he took up the receiver, before it could awaken Susan who had gone to bed early, after a hectic day of housecleaning, the results of which, he had to admit, were barely discernible.

"Dr. Prescott speaking," he said into the telephone.

"Dr. Prescott," it was Laura's voice, startling in its swift urgency, its frantic anxiety. "I know it's a foul night and it's a terrible imposition for me to dare call you—but—it's my sister—my baby sister—she's terribly ill—and I'm —so frightened—" her voice broke in a sob and Steve spoke swiftly.

"I'll come immediately," he assured her and put down the telephone.

He paused only long enough to scribble down the tele-

22

phone number of Laura's apartment, where he could be reached by Susie if there should be a call for him before he returned.

He let the car roll soundlessly down to the street before he switched on the motor, hoping that thus Susie would not be awakened by the noise.

It was after midnight and there was almost no traffic. With his doctor's insignia on the car, he drove as fast as he dared to the big apartment house.

Laura opened the door to him, her face white and innocent of make-up. He saw that she was shaking as though with cold, though the apartment was bright and warm. Her brocaded housecoat had long sleeves that buttoned to the cuffs and the bodice was zipped up to her chin.

"I—have to tell you, before you see her, Steve," she stammered and seemed completely unconscious that she had used his first name. "It's—pretty ghastly and I'm afraid you'll be—shocked. My—my sister is not quite eighteen—and unmarried—but—she has—had a child—she's—been brutally handled and I'm—frightened—"

She caught her breath and suddenly she was clinging to him, her face hidden against him, and she was stammering, "Oh, Steve, Steve—you've g-g-got to help her—you've g-g-got to—"

Steve's face was grim and hard.

"Was it—an illegal operation?" he demanded sharply.

"Oh, no! Steve—no!" she seemed shocked and acutely distressed. "What a horrible thing to ask! No, of course not—it—has been placed for adoption. Louise went to a private maternity hospital, where they—provide homes for the babies—"

"One of those 'black market in babies' places?" Steve's face was stiff with angry distaste.

"Steve, she's only a kid—she didn't know what to do. The man is married, very prominent, quite well-to-do. He wanted her to—destroy the baby but she wouldn't—the poor child came here, and hid. When the time came for the baby to be born, she was afraid to go to a hospital here in town—afraid I'd find out—the poor kid! If only she'd let me know! But she was frightened—"

"You have the address, of course," stated Steve flatly. "We'll hand it over to the police in the morning—"

"Oh, no! She'd have to testify. She's gone through so much, Steve, to keep anyone from knowing—we can't force her out into the open now. She'd be disgraced—ruined. I believe she'd kill herself."

Her shaking voice dropped almost to a whisper at the thought and Steve felt her trembling and realized for the first time that she was in his arms. He put her away from him sternly and said curtly, "Well, if she is in such bad shape, we'd better have a look at her and argue about the rest later," he said and moved purposefully towards the bedroom door.

The girl lay in bed, her shining blonde hair spread against the pillow, her face pinched and blue-white, wet with sweat, her eyes dark with pain. She seemed barely aware of Steve as he stood beside the bed, but she gave a small, sick moan and put her arm over her face as he began his examination.

Laura stood anxiously on the other side of the bed, watching him, sick with worry. When Steve had finished his examination, he faced her sternly.

"Such butchery as has been done on this child should be punished by hanging," he said through his teeth. "You must give me the name of the place. There couldn't have been a doctor or even a nurse in attendance—it's outrageous!"

Laura cringed and her tongue touched her lips as though to moisten them before she could speak, her voice husky, shaken, "Will she—will she—live?"

"Barring any unexpected complications—I suppose so," said Steve grimly. "But after the way she has been mistreated, she can never have another child."

"I'm so glad!" said Laura savagely.

Startled at the vehemence in her speech, Steve protested harshly, "That's a hideous thing to say—bearing children is a woman's most precious fulfillment."

Laura sneered. "The perfect family man, Doctor?" she said thinly, and her eyes, bright, derisive, bitter, met his straightly for a moment before she lowered the white lids that protected her from his stern gaze and said softly, "I wonder whether, after what she's been through, she would think so."

"Probably not, poor little devil," Steve agreed reluctantly. "If these kids had any sense—sense enough to realize the flaming danger of fooling around with sex, experimenting—"

"Then they wouldn't be kids, would they, Doctor?" Laura reminded him curtly and again for just a moment, she let him look into her eyes and see there something that made her seem a stranger.

Puzzled, his eyes probed hers curiously and suddenly color poured into her face. She looked away from him, putting a hand to her tumbled, shining curls that were in becoming disorder.

"I must look a sight," she stammered. "I was so frightened—"

"You know, of course, that the proper place for your sister is a hospital," Steve pointed out curtly.

Laura quailed as though he had plunged his fist against her jaw, and her eyes were dark with terror.

"Oh, no! No!" she stammered wildly. "Somebody would be sure to find out about what's happened. And when she's risked her life to keep her secret safe—Oh, you mustn't think about it any more. I can take care of her now."

Steve had expected nothing else, though his jaw set hard and grim and his eyes were cold.

"I can't insist on dragging her to the hospital against your will, of course," he admitted his helplessness. "I'll drop in tomorrow after office hours to have a look at her, and of course I won't expect you at the office tomorrow—" he was busily writing a prescription as he spoke.

"Oh, I'll come to the office, Doctor," she assured him quickly. "I have a friend, a nurse who is just off a case and who wants a few days rest before she takes another. She'll come in and look after Louise while I'm at the office."

Steve nodded grimly, too disgusted with the whole situation to offer argument he already knew would be futile.

He offered to drop off the prescriptions at an all-night drugstore that would make deliveries and said a curt good night.

Driving home, his mouth was twisted with anger and bitterness. These "private nursing homes" operating without a license, without supervision of any kind, hidden, secret from the police or other authorities, were damnable things. Girls like this Louise, frightened and bewildered by the consequences of their "love affairs," anxious only to be rid of the babies, caring nothing about what happened to them once they were free of them, were such pitiful victims. Yet victims whose own fear of discovery made it possible for the "maternity homes" to flourish and to charge outrageous rates.

Babies brought an excellent price on the "black market," as he and all other doctors knew. It was to the advantage of the "maternity homes" to look after the babies; many couples, for one reason or another denied children through the accredited welfare agencies, would pay well for a baby to be smuggled out of town and to some distant city, where they need only announce to their friends that they had adopted a baby. It was a "black market" that all decent people loathed and that welfare agencies, law enforcement officers and reputable physicians tried to fight. But it was like fighting smoke. Once in a great while, a "maternity home" was discovered, now and then a prosecuting witness could be persuaded to testify and the operators were sent away to prison; but for each one that was discovered, Steve knew there were a dozen that flourished handsomely. They charged enormous fees to the hapless unmarried mother; as much as the traffic would bear to the adopting "parents." And those who would protect the mothers from the sort of butchery this poor little devil had endured, were powerless to defend them because the very desperation that had sent the girls to the illegal "maternity homes" in the first place sealed their lips against any revelations that would have helped destroy the evil.

It was a long time, that night, before Steve could compose himself to the sleep his tired body needed so badly.

4. Poppa Spank

IT WAS NOT TO BE A FULL NIGHT'S sleep for Doctor Prescott. The shrill clanging of the phone by the bed made that obvious. Steve's groggy "Hello" was followed by a wide-awake "Be right over."

He left the rumpled bed and the half-asleep Susie and headed for his clothes.

"Where to?" Susie murmured, arm over her eyes.

"The Dalmoris. Something's wrong with the eldest daughter."

"Drive carefully, dear." Susie turned over drowsily.

Steve walked to the bed, leaned down and placed a tender kiss on each closed eyelid. Susie's face changed by a slight and sleepy contented smile. Steve, noticing this, smiled himself and brought his lips over the bridge of her nose and down to her lips which he lightly kissed. On impulse, he moved the blanket away from her body. The restlessness of sleep had made the ridiculous nightie she wore almost worthless; it had slipped from her shoulders and moved up from her legs.

Delighted and warmed by the sight, Steve bent his head and brushed the tip of her breast.

"Mmmm," she murmured and, eyes still closed, turned on her back and reached up, pulling Steve more closely to her. She raised his head from her breasts, opened her wet lips slightly and brought his mouth to her.

The kiss which followed carried desire in a warm rush through Steve; the movement of his hands made it apparent that he was becoming less and less willing to take on the starched and formal role of "Doctor Prescott."

Susie moved her mouth away and, with a light flick of her tongue on his lips, said, "Duty calls, dear. 'Bye." She pulled the blankets up under her chin.

27

Steve kissed her ear, tongue playing lightly and moving down her neck.

Suddenly Susie pulled an arm out from under the covers; one quick motion followed and Steve found himself sitting, very startled, on the floor.

"Hey!"

Susie turned over. "I'm tired, lover. Remember Hippocrates' oath. 'Sides, go make money." Her head disappeared under the blankets.

"Tease. That's all you are. Just a little tease." Steve stood up; grinning, he began to dress.

He stripped off his pajamas and walked around the room, collecting his clothes.

Susie peeped out from under the covers. "Wow, man," she said, "you've got a mark on your behind." She added, pulling up the blankets again, "You better see a doctor." With that, she disappeared.

Steve laughed aloud. My God, I love her, he thought— and then the image of Laura Weston crossed his mind. The image was followed by resolve: he would never see her any more, even talk to her, on a social, non-professional basis.

Rapidly he finished dressing in the semi-darkness of the room. His movements were swift and efficient, as though repetition had made each step of the process a reflex. Finally, dressed and ready to leave, he went to the bed again. Pulling the covers down slightly, he kissed Susie on the forehead.

"I love you," he said.

"I know," she nodded. "Hurry back, my darling."

With a deep breath of resignation, Steve pulled away from his wife and left the house.

The car, as usual, was facing the roadway; in moments, Dr. Steve Prescott was on his way to the emergency call.

The trip was a fairly long one, and the streets being nearly empty of traffic, Steve had much opportunity to think. Inevitably, his mind went back to the incident of the evening before. He thought of the poor stricken girl whose body had been so terribly butchered. He felt professional rage at that butchering, because it was completely inexcusable; the operation was a minor one, and only a sadistic fool or a drunken ass could have messed it up so badly.

Besides that, Steve felt guilty about not having taken the girl to a hospital; if she died, he knew he would feel more than a little responsible. He understood the shame she felt, and the deep fear, and he could conceive of the disgrace the family would feel if they knew what she had done. But the simple human aspects of the situation were much more important than the social ones—her life must take precedence over any unbending moral judgment. With an abrupt nod, Steve decided that if the girl were not considerably better today, he would force Laura to permit him to take her to a hospital.

Reassured, he pushed down on the accelerator and hurried toward his emergency call.

The Dalmori family inhabited a fine dwelling on a proud lane; in the early morning grayness, the trees seemed to stand like the storied defenders of a maiden's virtue. The house itself was full of light as he drove up. Turning off the ignition, he saw that Mr. and Mrs. Dalmori were standing in the open doorway, waiting for him.

"Doctor . . ."

The sound, virtually a plea, came from Mr. Dalmori. He was a big man, not so much tall as broad and much too well-fleshed; his distended and flabby belly came almost to his knees. The multi-colored pattern of his dressing gown seemed garishly overblown as it encircled his girth.

Mrs. Dalmori, hands clenched, waited in tears, her tiny face peering from behind her husband's expanse.

"Good morning," Steve said, wide awake and professional.

Mr. Dalmori leaned forward and gripped Steve's arm. The hammy palm was surprisingly strong, and Steve felt a definite twinge of annoyance.

"Doctor," the man burst forth, "you must not tell anyone." The grip hardened, and the man actually began to shake Steve. "You must not tell anyone why you are here, Doctor."

"The shame—" Mrs. Dalmori bleated from behind her husband.

"What is the mat . . ." Steve did not finish.

"I will not let you in my house, Doctor, unless you promise, you swear, not to say a word, not to whisper this shame, not to tell anyone this—this vile . . ." Speech seemed to fail him, but not strength. Wordlessly staring into Steve's face, his grip did not lessen in the slightest. Steve felt definitely bruised.

"Mr. Dalmori, please—" the man let go. "Thank you. Now, may I see your daughter?"

The three entered the hallway of the Dalmori household. There were numerous children standing at the top of the stairs, waiting curiously to inspect the visitor. At a gesture from Mr. Dalmori, they vanished. They vanished but not silently, and the racket of hurrying feet on the second floor made Steve try to remember just how many children the Dalmoris did have.

"Beatrice is in there." Mrs. Dalmori pointed a tiny finger toward a closed door.

Steve looked at her—the little woman's eyes were red and swollen and her hand trembled like a palsied leaf. For a moment, he thought of giving her a mild sedative— the daughter was probably in better condition than her mother, he judged, at least mentally—but then dismissed the notion.

He moved toward the closed door of the patient's room, but suddenly found his path thoroughly obstructed by the mass of Mr. Dalmori. Steve closed his eyes in great annoyance, opened them and said, "Mr. Dalmori, I have been called to see someone who is ill. You, in fact, were the one who called me. Now, why are you preventing me from getting to her?"

"Promise." Mr. Dalmori spoke a command.

Steve's annoyance grew to anger. "Promise what?" he snapped.

"You will not tell a soul what is wrong with my daughter."

"Are you sure that it's so terrible?"

Mrs. Dalmori moaned behind Steve; Mr. Dalmori drew

fat lids over egg-shaped eyes and slowly raised and lowered his head.

"I am sure," the fat man said positively.

"A doctor is sworn to keep patients' confidences, Mr. Dalmori."

Apparently satisfied, the bulk moved aside and Steve opened the door. He found himself in the living room.

There was a flurry of movement, a short squeal, and much tugging and wrapping of floral drapes around two bodies huddled in opposite corners of the room.

Dr. Prescott blinked. Then the whole thing suddenly struck him as funny; it was with great effort that he did not cry, "Come out, come out, wherever you are!"

"No, you do not come in." Mr. Dalmori was pushing his wife back into the hall. Weight, if not authority, made battle impossible and he succeeded, slammed the door and bolted it. He turned to face the room.

"Beatrice!" he boomed.

There was no motion, but Dr. Prescott did hear a thin whine: "Father, please . . ."

"Beatrice, come!"

Steve watched in fascination as the robin's-egg blue floral drape, lumped in the corner, hesitantly shifted its position. The bulk beneath the drape made no attempt to stand, but as soon as Mr. Dalmori made one monumental move in that direction, the drapery rose and half-exposed the body of a very young and very frightened girl. Clumsily holding the covering about her body, she stumbled toward her father.

5. That's His Problem

"**T**HIS IS MY SHAME." MR. DALMORI grabbed his daughter's arm and pulled her before the doctor. She stood, head hanging, in complete silence.

"Is she ill?" Dr. Prescott asked.

"Ill? She is—she is—" In rage, he shook the girl violently. "She is rotten!"

Steve noticed that she was trembling. "What is the matter?" he asked, more to her as reassurance than to her father.

"See if she is pregnant, Doctor." He thrust the girl from him. Her head snapped back and Steve saw fury and hatred flick across her eyes.

Steve motioned toward the couch and watched the girl as, holding her unwieldy gown, she walked awkwardly across the room and sat down clumsily. The leg accidentally exposed was young, firm and lovely—Steve could not help noticing that.

"Well, Doctor?" Mr. Dalmori loomed ominously in front of him. "Examine."

"What makes you think the poor thing is pregnant? And is that what you called me for at this hour of the morning?"

A red flush started across the girl's cheeks, and when the tears began to fall, she curled back on the couch as if trying to hide herself.

Her father glared at her for a long silent minute before he spoke; when he did speak at last, his voice was harsh and grating with fury.

"Where is he?" the father demanded.

Dr. Prescott looked around him and realized that the shivering mass of floral drapery in the other corner of the room must be the "he" Mr. Dalmori had just refused to designate by name. A smile started across his face as he put the pieces of this "emergency call" together and he had to suppress an impulse to laugh aloud.

Mr. Dalmori was standing before the form on the floor. He gave the floral mass a solid kick in what was probably the rump and the mass leaped up with a yowl to stand very tall, very male, and very naked. He fumbled toward the cloth lying near his feet, but Mr. Dalmori gave him no chance. The man planted a beefy hand on the nape of the boy's neck and dragged him toward Dr. Prescott.

Nude, beet red, the boy stood in trembling fear and embarrassment before the doctor. He flailed helplessly to cover his nakedness, gave up and stood quiet, hands tight to his sides, fists clenched, eyes squeezed shut.

By this time, Beatrice had screamed and her father had shouted, "Shut up!"

Steve so far had not laughed, or even smiled, but the boy's request now almost broke his control. Through tight lips and clenched teeth, the lad said, "Sir, please ask him to return my trousers."

Mr. Dalmori gave the good doctor no time to reply. "This thing," he said, tone taut with anger, "is why you must examine my daughter. This—this animal!"

If this sad creature is an animal, Steve thought, noting the knobby knees and shaking legs, he's not much more than an infant doe.

"Mr. Dalmori," Steve said, thinking to try the rational, "even if your daughter is pregnant, I couldn't possibly tell this soon after—"

The fat man spun and pointed the finger of wrath at his daughter. "Examine her!"

"Now, Mr. Dalmori," Steve began, "don't you think—"

"Doctor, please make him give me my trousers, please!"

"Shut up, you filthy—"

"Father, leave him alone!"

"You keep quiet!"

"Beatrice, don't—"

"Now wait," Steve started. "I suggest—"

"Father, I didn't—"

"Didn't? Didn't? I saw you! I saw! Trash! Garbage! Filth!"

"Sir, we didn't—"

"I saw! I saw!"

"Oh, Father!"

The cry rose to a wail, the wail to a wracking yell, the wracking yell to a shriek—a shrill and rhythmic "Oh, oh, oh, oh!"

Mr. Dalmori responded by seizing his daughter and tearing the covering material away from her body. Her hands went over her eyes and she sat in total shame, knees slightly bent, her nakedness complete, her body young, fresh, and unsensual. The shrieks had stopped, and so had the trembling, but the incredible flesh of Mr. Dalmori quivered and shook before his daughter.

"Aiiee!"

This from the girl as the crack of his powerful hand against her face shattered through the room. He drew back his arm to strike again, but Steve grabbed his wrist.

"Stop that, Mr. Dalmori!"

The fat face turned to Steve; the look was one of fury and incomprehension.

"Stop?" he said. "Stop? Stop what? Does she deserve less?" His voice rose. "A whip, a whip! That she deserves. Disgrace, the disgrace to me—" He whirled toward the boy.

"And him? Him!" In a swift step, he had the boy by the shoulder. "You—you think maybe you get better? It's easier, maybe, because you had some fun? Fun!" He spat the word. "You think you are a man, hey? A man?" He moved his head close to the other's white face. "And if you have brought shame to this house, you will be not a man when you leave it." He brought his balled fist hard against the boy's groin.

The youth slumped to the floor in a faint.

Steve went to Mr. Dalmori and put a hand on his shoulder.

"Sit down. We will go on with the examination when you sit down."

Dalmori placed himself in a wing chair that faced the

window and sat so, in silence, his back to his sobbing daughter and the prostrate boy.

"Mr. Dalmori, where are the young man's clothes?"

There was no response.

"Mr. Dalmori, nothing can be done until the boy is dressed. Where are his things?"

The answer was a gesture toward the closed and locked door.

Steve unbolted the door and swung it open—and there was Mrs. Dalmori, tears running down her cheeks, holding a collection of rumpled clothing in her arms.

She extended the pile to Steve and said, voice thin and shaking, "He has a bad temper. He is like—like fire, like an animal. He cannot stop." Steve took the clothing from her and she looked him full in the face. "Please forgive—" She stopped herself; the shrug was a gesture of profound resignation and weariness.

With that she stepped back and he closed the door.

Steve went to work on reviving the boy, who still lay unconscious on the floor. When he stirred with a faint moan, Steve spoke to him. He told him to dress, to leave the room, but not under any circumstances to leave the house; he was to wait in the hall until told otherwise.

When the door closed once again, Steve looked at Mr. Dalmori; the man yet sat in the wing chair, his back to the room, staring out of the window now lit by dawn. Steve turned to the girl.

She sat, covered once more, and watched Steve. Her eyes were swollen and red but they were dry. One cheek was puffed and livid from her father's blow.

Steve smiled at her, took the necessary instruments from his bag, and explained carefully that the examination would be brief and that he would not hurt her. She did not speak or respond in any way, and moved only as she was directed.

Finished, Steve covered her with the drape as well as he could. "You're all right," he said.

She nodded curtly. "I know."

Curious suddenly, he asked, "How old are you?"

"Seventeen."

He shook his head. "Well," he said, "I'm going to give you an injection that will let you sleep for several hours. An ice bag will take down the swelling on that cheek."

He gave her the injection as she watched quietly, helped her to her feet and walked with her to the door.

In the hallway, the boy sat dejectedly on a straight-back chair near an umbrella stand. He raised his head sharply as the door opened, but Steve motioned for him to remain where he was. Mrs. Dalmori came in, hurried and haggard, from a room in the back. As she approached Steve, question on her face, he smiled reassuringly and nodded.

"She's perfectly all right," he said. "Now, let her get some sleep—I've given her something that will help. And an ice bag or some ice in a towel would help her cheek, too. Don't worry, Mrs. Dalmori."

The little woman smiled in gratitude. "Come, Beatrice," she said, taking her daughter by the arm. "To bed now."

Listlessly, the girl went up the stairs with her mother.

Steve turned to the boy. "You do have a name, don't you?"

"Yes, sir. Warren."

"All right, Warren. I'll . . . Say, don't I know you from somewhere?"

Warren flushed. "Yes, Dr. Prescott. I'm an orderly at the hospital. I've seen you there lots of times."

"Well, that's not important now. I'll be finished here in a few more minutes. Then I'll drive you home."

"Yes, sir," Warren nodded.

Steve went back into the living room. As he expected, the bulk of Mr. Dalmori sat slumped in the chair.

"I'm finished, Mr. Dalmori. I thought you would like to know that your daughter is all right. She is not pregnant. She is still a virgin."

At that, the fat man raised his head and looked into Dr Prescott's face. Then his eyes filled with tears.

Steve picked up his bag and coat and left the room. Warren beside him, he drove away from the Dalmori household in the full light of early morning.

6. Private Room

THEY DROVE IN SILENCE FOR SEV-
eral minutes. Finally, Steve spoke.

"Well, Warren, just what did happen in there?"

The boy shifted uncomfortably. "You see, sir, we were
—uh—we were just necking, and you know, things got a
little, well, a little further than usual and so we thought
we would—" He stopped abruptly. "Sir, I mean nothing
would have happened, I wouldn't ever have made her do
anything. She's a nice girl, sir, I know that."

"Warren, just tell me what happened."

"Yes, sir. Well, we were necking and, as I said, we
went pretty far. So we—well, you saw how we were. Her
folks were out and we sort of lost track of time—you know
how it is. Well, and then Mr. Dalmori called you. Doctor," Warren was suddenly serious, "is he crazy or something?"

"No," Steve answered. "He just loves his daughter a
little too much. And there are a lot of things he doesn't
understand."

The boy nodded glumly.

"Warren," Steve said a few minutes later, "tell me to
shut up if you want, but have you ever made love to a
woman? I mean, full love?"

"Oh, yes, sir." Warren spoke proudly. "I certainly have."
His tone suggested a Casanova-like history.

"Oh?"

"Yes." Warren slumped back against the seat. "Oh,
hell, Dr. Prescott, I mean I have, sure, but it hasn't been
much good. No moonlight and roses or anything like that.
In fact, when you get right down to it, the whole thing
was pretty lousy."

"Prostitutes?"

"No. It was just once, Dr. Prescott, that's all. In the hospital."

"Nurse?"

"No, sir." The boy seemed embarrassed. "One of the patients."

Steve nodded, uncommenting, eyes on the road. "Want to tell me how it happened? Any particular reason why it was so bad?"

"I don't mind talking about it if you want to hear." Warren paused. "You know, Dr. Prescott, when you think about it, what happened is pretty funny. It was with a girl who had six toes."

"What?" Steve laughed.

"Yeah, she had six toes on one foot—the left, I think. She was in the hospital to have it cut off. . . ."

Warren told how he had been on night duty in the private wing of the hospital. Pushing his orderly cart before him through the halls, he felt more bored than usual; nearly all of the patients were asleep, and the night nurse was a bitch, interested only in the interne on duty.

Warren went from room to room, emptied ashtrays, closed or opened curtains, shut off lights, filled water pitchers.

In Room 809, he found an old and very wrinkled woman lying calmly asleep on the bed. Her hair was tied neatly back with a colorful scarf, and her small hand lay gracefully upon the book she must have been reading when she had fallen asleep. Approaching to remove the book, Warren noted that she looked like a pleasant person, not the usual old-biddy type that sent groans of perpetual complaint through the hospital all day and all night.

Standing by the bed, Warren looked curiously at the woman's form outlined by the single sheet drawn over her body.

"She's had sex," he nodded solemnly to himself.

He looked carefully into her face and at the contours of her body and went off into a long stream of speculation about whether she had been a virgin on her wedding night; then he wondered about her extra-marital affairs. Before long, speculation had turned to fantasy and Warren, thoroughly aroused, had constructed a complete history of the elderly woman's sex life when she had been a girl and even how she had behaved in bed.

He put the book on the night table, filled the water pitcher, and turned off the light. Tugging his white jacket down, he left the room.

The next few visits were uneventful; nothing happened to distract Warren's thoughts from matters of the flesh. When he entered 822, he jumped with surprise at seeing a feminine figure sitting in the visitor's chair.

It was a young woman in her late twenties, perhaps early thirties. Her face was not unattractive, but there was a look of tiredness and long-held petulance to its expression. She appeared quite healthy in silk pajamas and Mandarin robe. Her voice was high-pitched and tense.

"Oh, I'm glad to see you. I don't like being alone before my operation. I'm sorry, but I just can't stand being alone before an operation. It's rude of me to be so silly, but I can't bear being alone." She expelled a huge breath. "Can you stay here and talk to me for a while?"

Warren checked down the hall—the night nurse was walking toward her desk, clipboard in hand.

"Yes," he answered. "The nurse just made her rounds." He lit a cigarette and offered one to her, which she declined with a nervous wave of the hand.

"You seem pretty healthy," Warren said. "Mind if I ask what you're here for?"

She pointed. "That's why."

Warren noticed for the first time that she wore only one sock; her right foot was bare in the slipper, her left covered by thin white cotton.

"What's the matter with it?"

She sighed deeply and hesitated. "It's abnormal. I have—" the pause was brief— "I have an extra toe on that foot."

Warren laughed aloud. "Is that all?"

"All?" She was aghast. "All?"

Leaning forward in her chair, she delivered a lengthy harangue about the horrors of being born with an extra toe. It was obvious that she held that tiny appurtenance responsible for her unpopularity with women, animals, children, God and, of course, men—in that order.

The tirade of self-pity ended with a query: "Could you love a girl who was abnormal like me?"

Warren recognized the question as a plea and as an opportunity; his heart thumped. The words of his quick reply created in him an impulse to laugh, but she took them very seriously: "I could love a girl with six toes on both feet."

The woman looked intently at him. "Could you?"

"Yes."

"I don't believe you."

"It's the truth."

She rose from the chair and sat down on the bed. "I don't believe it."

"I can prove it."

"Can you?"

"Yes."

"How?"

"Like this." Warren drew the curtains around the bed, enclosing the girl and himself in the small area. His movements were calm, but his heart pounded and real fear moved in his veins.

He turned and saw that the girl had lain back on the bed and was watching him, lids lowered. Her robe was parted, the pajama coat unbuttoned.

"Like this," he said again, and went to her, the unfulfilled desire of eighteen years forcing fear aside.

The boy and the woman, gasping and straining, fumbled with each other's bodies. Warren soon realized that she was as much a virgin as he.

Quickly, he was done and moved away from her.

She lay with her eyes closed, her teeth clamped down hard on her lower lip. Warren did not know what to say. He slid his hand down over her damp body, paused to caress the breasts, and suddenly started to laugh.

"Oh, Jesus!"

Her eyes flew open, alive with fury. "What are you laughing at?"

"I'm sorry, I'm really sorry, but—but—" Warren could not finish; he pointed.

Amid her complaisant nudity, after the frantic incoherence of sex, the sight was too much: the sock on her left foot rose in a neat line to the middle of her calf, there to be topped by a small meticulous cuff, capped by a fluffy and undisturbed red bow.

"Oh, Jesus. It never even got mussed . . ."

The girl began to laugh, too. In a moment, both Warren and she were roaring affectionately, happily. At that moment, the night nurse looked in to see what all the noise was about . . .

"I nearly lost my job," Warren said.

Steve was laughing heartily. "That patient sounds very sad, of course, the unfortunate thing. I'm glad you were able to give her such good pre-operative preparation." He burst out laughing again. "But after all, a sixth toe is not a tragedy."

"Oh, if she thought so, then it was—" Warren was grinning, too.

"Warren, I must say that your sex life is beginning to sound like a musical comedy. The risqué kind."

"Beg pardon, Dr. Prescott?"

"Never mind. Well, here we are." Steve pulled up in front of Warren's home and turned to the boy. "Keep way from fat fathers and two-headed dogs, lad."

The two men smiled at each other and Steve drove off, still laughing aloud.

7. Second Visit

LAURA WAS WAITING FOR HIM IN the office when he arrived the next morning, and she was pale, and there were faint smudges beneath her eyes as though she had not slept.

In his private office as she took his hat and coat from him and hung them up, he asked grimly, "How is your sister this morning?"

Laura turned swiftly and there was a stain of color in her cheeks and her eyes were uneasy.

"She's much better, thank you, Doctor," her voice was low, not quite steady. "You know, I'm sure, that you have put me under an obligation that I will never be able to repay."

She came to the edge of his desk, looking down at him and he was conscious of a faint fragrance like that of a summer garden, dew-wet, that brushed him lightly and was gone almost before he could be sure that he had experienced it at all.

"I shall be grateful to you as long as I live, Doctor," she told him huskily. "There is nothing you could ask of me that I would not gladly do to prove that to you."

Steve's jaw was set and hard.

"I'll take you up on that," he stated flatly. "Tell me the name and address of this—butcher-shop—"

Laura took a single backward step and the lovely color drained from her face and there was a flicker that was close to panic in her eyes.

"That's—something I can't tell you—" she stammered faintly.

Steve's eyes were bitterly derisive, his voice cutting.

"You're so grateful to me you'd do anything I asked—

except the one helpful thing, not only for your sister but for all girls like her. You refuse," he said harshly.

"I can't tell you, because—I don't know," said Laura hurriedly and would not meet his eyes. He knew she was lying. "She wouldn't tell me."

"You are a nurse and so you know what places of horror these establishments are—you know, too, that the only way they can be put out of business is for their victims to report them—"

"Any woman desperate enough to need the services of such a place would be too desperate to risk telling anything," she flung at him hotly, holding her voice low by an obvious effort. "Don't you see, Steve? In order to—close up these places, the victims must go into court and testify—"

"Arrangements could be made to have them testify in secret, their identities protected—" began Steve.

"Do you think my sister—or any woman—would take such a chance? They're like frightened, trapped animals, wanting only to get out of the trap. They would rather die ten times over, as my sister would have died without your help, than to run the risk of being discovered."

Steve had expected nothing else, even when he had started the interrogation, and he made a little weary gesture. He was so disgusted and troubled that he did not realize she had called him "Steve" instead of her customary formal "Doctor."

"What happened to the baby? Born dead, I suppose," he said.

"Oh, no—it was a fine healthy baby—a boy. It was adopted by some fine people—" said Laura hastily.

"Fine people who are willing to take the risk of adopting a baby from such a place?" demanded Steve.

Laura colored and her eyes fell away from his.

"I imagine it's a comforting thought," he growled, and dismissed the subject and said curtly, "Let's get started with the day's work."

As she reached the door, her hand on the knob, he asked casually, yet his eyes sharp, "Oh, by the way—do you happen to know a Dr. Anna Harmon?"

Laura's back was rigid, and it was an instant before she turned to face him, her face quite pale, her head up.

"I suppose Dr. Hurst had to—spill his guts," she said viciously, and set her teeth hard in her lower lip. "Well, I do know Anna—and she had a raw deal from the hospital. She went to pieces after she was held accountable for something she did not do. The crime belonged to one of the house doctors. But because Anna was only an interne, it was easier for the hospital to slough it off on her and make an example of her—"

"I cannot believe that, Laura," he snapped.

"I suppose not," she said dryly and there was a stinging lash in her voice. "All male doctors resent feminine doctors and will stop at nothing to discredit them—"

"I suppose Dr. Harmon is back of one of these 'maternity homes'," said Steve shrewdly, and saw the flash of panic deepen in her eyes.

"That's not true," she flashed at him hotly. "Anna's not even in town. She's gone north. She's employed in a research laboratory."

"Good," said Steve, not believing her for a moment. "I'm glad to know that. And now we'll have the first patient in, please."

Laura stood for a moment against the closed door, watching him, her eyes frightened. She turned with a defiant jerk of her lovely head and opened the door.

Later in the evening, after he had completed his rounds of calls, Steve went up in the elevator to Laura's apartment and rang the bell. She opened the door for him, cool and immaculate and very lovely in a honey-yellow taffeta housecoat that was a perfect foil for her shining hair and her lovely skin. Her eyes were anxious and uneasy as she greeted him and showed him immediately into the bedroom.

Steve stood beside the bed, looking down at the girl who lay there, so small and slight that her body seemed scarcely to disturb the covers. Her eyes were closed, and the long lashes lay against purplish shadows beneath her eyes that were like bruises. And as he stood looking down at her, the lashes lifted and the girl's eyes stared up at him and there was fear and something very like hatred in her eyes. For a long moment she met his gaze, her thin, colorless mouth taut, before she put up her arm to hide her face and submit wordlessly to the examination he must make.

He nodded to Laura when he had completed his examination. The girl kept her face covered by her arm. He turned and went out of the room, Laura following him.

"She's better, isn't she?" asked Laura anxiously.

"She's showing satisfactory progress but she's not yet out of the woods," stated Steve. "A narrow squeak. There is still danger. And I still say the proper place for her is a hospital."

"That's—impossible," said Laura.

Steve nodded, because he hadn't expected her to say anything else.

"Of course, if she dies, you know that you and I will be guilty of criminal negligence," he pointed out.

"Oh, but she's not going to—because you are taking care of her," said Laura and her relief and gratitude made her suddenly radiant.

"That's very flattering," said Steve grimly. "And of course I'm a fool not to insist on the hospital—"

Laura came close to him and from the whispering taffeta of her housecoat there floated up to him for a tantalizing moment that faint fragrance of a dew-wet summer garden.

"No, darling," she said very softly, so softly that he could almost convince himself she had not spoken the endearment at all. "You're very kind and very wise and very—sweet—as I knew you would be."

And suddenly, impulsively, almost as though scarcely aware of what she was doing, Laura kissed him full on the mouth. Kissed him warmly, as though she had wanted very much to do so for a long time but had lacked the courage. And the next moment she stood back, color pouring into her face, and said unsteadily, "I—that was unforgivable. But I'm so grateful. You're such a wonderful person—"

She walked with him to the door and swung it open,

and as he brushed past her she said very softly, "Good night—darling—my darling."

Going down in the elevator, Steve found himself worried and uneasy. He had a healthy, normal disgust for a doctor who took advantage of his position to have an affair with his office nurse. It was the same principle as that of a business man having an affair with his secretary, a man who used his position as employer to demand of his employee services far beyond those included in the paycheck. There had never for a moment been an instant's temptation for him; he had young, pretty, impressionable nurses, girls with their "R.N." pins shiny-new, the ink scarcely dry on their diplomas, who were seeking experience before deciding between private duty and hospital service. He had never had any feeling towards any of them except an almost fatherly one. But Laura was something else again. She was no starry-eyed kid, still jubilant over the acquisition of her cherished cap and her precious pin; Laura was a woman, mature, subtle, dangerous. The word "dangerous" startled him, and he slowed the car, frowning as he turned the word over and over in his mind. Dangerous? To whom? She was a darned alluring, very tempting woman—but—Susie was his wife; there were the two boys; his home; all the things he held dear. Were they not a shield, armor in fact, against even such a woman as Laura? Well— *weren't they?* He was oddly uneasy at the sudden vehemence of his thoughts on the subject. It relieved him greatly when he reached the driveway in front of the white brick ranch-house and the two boys rushed out to greet him. Now he could free himself from disturbing thoughts.

But somehow, tonight of all nights, he seemed to see Susie with a new and unwilling clarity. Her hair, which she always admitted frankly was just "hair-colored," was straight and she wore it thrust into an untidy knot pinned at the back. The easiest and quickest way she could get it out of her way when she awoke in the morning. She always went around shedding hairpins and thrusting them absent-mindedly into place. Tonight the knot was slipping; her face, innocent of any vestige of makeup, was flushed and damp from activities connected with Bill's party. Her house dress that had been immaculate some hours before now showed where one of the boys, with grubby small paws, had tugged at her skirt to attract her attention; she had spilled egg on the front of it while beating eggs for a cake, and had wiped it off with a damp cloth. There hadn't been time to change into another fresh dress before dinner. Besides, since she did the laundry herself each week, she was understandably chary about "breaking out" two freshly ironed house dresses in a single day.

Steve despised himself because suddenly, beside Susie's untidy, grubby little fingers, he seemed to see Laura, immaculate, exquisitely groomed, the whisper of scented taffeta skirts swirling about her high-heeled slippers, her lovely face touched artfully with makeup. And suddenly once more he felt the touch of her mouth, cool, fragrant, petal-soft, against his own—and drew a hard breath and cursed himself that he should think of such things here at the table with his wife and his two boys. Susie smiled radiantly at him across the table, sharing some joke about the boys, and he was stricken with remorse. Why shouldn't Susie look hot and rumpled and tired, after a day of riding herd on the boys? Minnie did the cooking and the housework; but Susie had her hands full, too. She scarcely left the house; she was always on hand to look after whatever telephone calls from patients came to the house, for one thing. It was a rare occasion indeed when she got together with some of the many friends who adored her; on the scarce nights when he and she could join friends, he could see how Susie was always the center of the gayest group at the party. People loved her because she was sweet and honest and gay and loyal to the teeth.

Loyal! He knew she would have died in any painful way that would have saved him a moment's discomfort. She worshipped him and the boys. Yet here he was, criticizing her, comparing her to a woman who had no demands on her time after office hours; nothing to do but make herself beautiful and glamorous. And a woman his instincts told him was very dangerous—a woman he must avoid in the future.

He reached the decision almost without being conscious of it. The decision that Laura must be discharged. He dared not run the risk of keeping her on at the office. He disliked the word "risk" and yet he was honest enough to realize that it was a truthful word.

8. Broken Faith

HE WAS A LITTLE LATE REACHING
the office next morning and there was no chance for a
private word with Laura. He felt that she would not
accept her dismissal calmly. He tried to deny that he was
secretly relieved at the postponement of an unpleasant
scene, and gave himself up to his usual busy routine. And
when he left the office at the end of the day, he still had
not brought up the subject. But he would be calling on old
Mrs. Logan this evening and would, of course, stop by to
check on Louise. And what better place was there to tell
Laura definitely and flatly that she was through as his
office nurse than in the privacy of her own apartment?

He was tight-lipped when he rang the bell at Laura's
apartment. She opened the door to him, distractingly lovely
in one of the clinging, soft housecoats that she seemed
invariably to choose for her evenings at home. She smiled
at him warmly and motioned him in with a gesture that
took in the table, already laid for two, the candles ready
for lighting and the pleasant fragrance of appetizing food
already present in the air.

She took his hat and coat and before he could speak,
she said gaily, "You see, I knew you were not expected
home for dinner and that you had had only a sandwich
and a glass of milk for lunch. So I planned this for you."

"Thanks," said Steve and could not quite keep the
grimness from his tone. "I'll see your sister first—"

"Oh, but—Louise is gone, Steve," said Laura and for
a moment her eyes flickered away from his.

"Gone?" he repeated, startled.

"She was getting along so well and she was homesick,
and a friend agreed to drive her home—" she explained
hastily.

49

"If you had told me that at the office this afternoon, I'd have been spared the drive out here," Steve told her curtly.

She stood before him, demure, a smile tugging at the corner of her mouth, her eyes dancing warmly.

"I know it, Steve," she admitted frankly. "But I wanted you to come. I wanted to talk to you—away from the office."

Steve studied her sharply.

"Perhaps it's just as well," he said. "Because I wanted to talk to you—away from the office."

She caught her breath and her eyes widened and there were little fans of carnation-pink in her cheeks for a moment.

"You did?" she breathed. "Oh, Steve—that's wonderful!"

He was very tired. It was a cold night. Susie was not expecting him for dinner because she knew that he would go straight from his calls to the hospital; and at the moment, he was ravenously hungry. Besides, wasn't this a much better opportunity for the talk he must have with Laura than to try to sandwich in a private moment or two at the office?

And so when Laura summoned him to the table, he sat down and ate the delicious food she served, and listened to her gay, carefree chatter and did not realize that the uneasiness in her eyes deepened as the meal progressed. When at last they had finished and cigarettes were lighted, he looked at her and knew the moment could be evaded no longer.

"Well, shall we talk?" he suggested curtly. "Will you start—or shall I?"

"Oh—you, by all means. I'm afraid what I have to say may not be nearly so important," she told him brightly.

He crushed out his cigarette in the tray she had placed beside his dinner cup and suddenly he looked up at her and delivered his blow.

"I'm going to have to ask you, Laura, to find another job."

She lowered her eyes and he saw the small ridge of

muscle that for an instant rippled along her jaw before she had herself once more under control.

"You're the sort of woman, Laura, who would be a menace to any wife's happiness—"

She looked up at him then and there was pain in her blue eyes.

"That sounds as though—you felt it, too," she said huskily.

His hand clenched hard on the edge of the table.

"Felt what, Laura?" he asked, and even in his own ears the words sounded silly and insane.

"I'm in love with you, darling," she said very softly. "For the first time in my life."

Steve thrust back his chair and stood up.

"That's not true, Laura."

Almost in a single graceful fluid movement she was on her feet and the table was no longer between them and from her soft satin draperies came that tantalizing, oddly disturbing flower-fragrance that was so much a part of her.

She was so close to him now that the flower-fragrance was all about him, bemusing him, drugging his senses, seeming to grow stronger with the added tension.

"It's quite true, Steve—why fight it, darling?" she murmured, and her voice was a siren-song in his ears. "I hate to sound corny, but the truest things in the world are corny—that's what makes people repeat them over and over so that they become corny. You know that we love each other, that what we feel for each other is much bigger than anything else in the world. Oh, darling, darling—I can give you so much—more than any other woman in the world. Because you're all my life—you're all I ever wanted—"

Steve took a backward step, a hand flung up to hold her back, his face gray and harsh in the flickering yellow candle-light.

"This is the most damnable nonsense, Laura. We mean nothing to each other," he told her shortly.

"We could, darling—we could! And what you would give me would take nothing from—her. Oh, Steve, Steve, don't be so hard! Don't torture me—and yourself. Don't deny us both this bit of perfect heaven! No one will ever know. And Steve, Steve darling, I love you so much. So terribly much—"

And then she was in his arms, held close and hard against him and everything was forgotten save that she was in every exquisite inch the fulfillment of any man's most ardent dreams; and she was his for the taking, and she gave herself with a joyous abandon, a prodigal display of emotion that set his blood singing as it had never sung before. It was an hour of such utter perfection as all men dream of and few men ever experience. Everything else was forgotten and when at last it was over, and she lay close-held in his arms, there was a small, satisfied smile on her lovely mouth and triumph in her eyes.

Bitter shame and self-loathing were pulling at Steve even while he dressed and made ready to leave her. Already an hour late for his hospital calls, but at the moment there was no room in his thoughts for that. He could only remember that he had been faithless to Susie, who would have staked her very life on his loyalty, who would no more have dreamed him capable of such betrayal than she herself could have been.

Laura lay against her pillows, the sheet carelessly drawn up so that her beautiful bust and white shoulders were quite bare, and watched him, tender, teasing amusement in her eyes.

"I—don't know what to say, Laura," he could not walk out without a word and yet words stuck in his throat, thickened with the bitter self-disgust of his betrayal of Susie's loyalty.

"Don't say anything, darling. It's not a time for words," she assured him softly. "You might kiss me good night."

But he turned sharply away and caught up his coat and hat and moved towards the door.

"Perhaps it's just as well," she laughed softly. "We can talk—later on."

He could not answer her. He let himself out of the apartment, closing the door hard behind him. And Laura, still propped against her pillows, suddenly turned her head until her laughter was smothered against the cool linen. But the look in her eyes gave the laughter an ugly inflection, for it was a look of malicious enjoyment, a look that boded no good to a bedeviled, bewitched and harassed young doctor who adored his wife and had never strayed from his marital vows until now.

9. Change of Heart

LAURA GREETED HIM DEMURELY
next morning when he entered the office. Demurely, save
for the small twinkle that was a teasing light in her eyes.
Her manner was quite perfect throughout the day but
when the last patient had gone, and they were alone, he
looked at her sternly.

"Sit down, Laura. We might as well have this out here
and now," he told her.

Laughter brimmed for a moment in her eyes but she was
still the polite, perfect office assistant.

"Hadn't I better lock the outer door, Doctor?" she asked
sweetly.

"That won't be necessary."

Her eyebrows went up and some of the teasing, mocking
laughter faded from her eyes as she sat primly, hands
folded in her lap, ankles neatly crossed, in the chair beside
his desk.

"Yes, Doctor?" she said, her whole manner making a
light mockery of her formality.

"I have a patient who is leaving the hospital tomorrow
and who will require the services of a skilled and efficient
nurse for at least two or three weeks," he stated. "I have
recommended you for the job."

All the mockery had gone now and for a moment there
was a spark of anger in her eyes.

"That's very kind of you, Doctor," she told him evenly.
"But I don't think I care to take on a private-duty case.
I'm much better satisfied here."

His jaw set.

"That's too bad," he answered grimly. "Because I
stopped in at the Registry this morning, and asked them
to send me a new office nurse. Fortunately for me they had

54

one available and she will report for duty in the morning."

"So I am to be punished for something we both enjoyed," she said harshly.

"I'm sorry it has to be like this—"

"Oh—sorry!" she flung the word at him like a blow. "What the hell good is that going to do? You were tickled to death to accept what I had to offer—now you're behaving like a silly school boy who for the first time has found out for himself some of the facts of life and is scared to death. You—a doctor, who should know just how unimportant such passionate interludes are."

Steve studied her coldly, shrewdly.

"If you consider it so unimportant, then why the fuss?" he demanded.

Instantly the cold anger went out of her and she was all soft and warm and appealing, and there was even something that dimmed the brightness of her eyes that in another woman he might have mistaken for tears.

"It wasn't unimportant to me, darling—it was just about the most important thing that ever happened—the most perfect! Because I love you." Her voice broke and for a moment she hid her face in her hands, and Steve could think of nothing to say that wouldn't sound completely banal and inane.

"I'm sorry," he muttered again. "But there isn't any other way—"

"Oh, I'll accept my dismissal," she told him bleakly. "Because there isn't anything else for me to do. There never is, for the 'woman scorned.' I'm being corny again, aren't I? But after all, what else is there but the truth—corny though it be? I gave you a gift that meant everything to me. But I can't force you to accept it if you no longer want it—only—darling, are you sure?"

"Very sure," Steve despised himself because his voice sounded unnecessarily harsh.

She stood quite still for a moment, studying him as curiously as if she had never seen him before. And then, to his startled surprise, she smiled. A small, provocative, almost teasing smile that whipped the blood to reluctant warmth.

"This isn't really goodbye, darling," she told him softly. "There never could be really a goodbye between us. Because you won't forget me, darling. Even in your lawful wedded bed, with her in your arms, you'll remember me. And want what I have to offer. Want it so much that you'll be sick with wanting it. And—I'll be waiting for you, darling. The gift will be yours again—any time, anywhere."

And before he could recover from the incredible effrontery of her words she was gone. He discovered he was trembling slightly and that he was sweating. . . .

Nurse Middleton was middle-aged, comfortably plump, frankly maternal in her attitude towards her new employer. From the first she was a distinctly soothing influence in the office. Her manner with children, terrified of the unknown things conjured up by "seeing the doctor," was perfect. She could be gently soothing and cheering to even the most convinced hypochondriacs. Her manner with those who were grievously ill and had faced up to it with courage was deeply touching.

Susie adored her at sight, and beamed happily at Steve on one of the infrequent visits she made to the office. Not demanding that she be allowed to see Steve the moment she arrived, Susie took her place with whatever patients were in the office and waited her turn, meanwhile watching Nurse Middleton appraisingly and approvingly.

"I'm mad about her, dear," she told Steve happily. "She'll take care of you. And I'm so glad you got rid of that lovely creature—she was too beautiful! No normal wife, especially one as homely and dull as I am, could ever approve of having her husband exposed to the charms of such a gal."

Steve caught her in his arms and held her tightly.

"Mind what you say about my favorite wife," he ordered sternly. "Remember, you're speaking of the woman I love."

"So long as you remember it, darling!" she warned

him, mocking, adoring, clinging to him shamelessly, and rubbing her cheek kittenwise against his shoulder.

"I promise you—I'll never forget it!" said Steve and his voice was deep and warm and vibrant. His words were an oath, a vow from the heart. . . .

He wondered, of course, what had happened to Laura. He heard nothing of her as he went his busy rounds, and finally decided that perhaps she had left town. Maybe she had joined her friend, Dr. Harmon, at that research laboratory up north. Wherever she was, he knew that she would be all right, for Laura had impressed him as a woman quite capable of taking care of herself.

Christmas came and went and it was a gay, happy season of noise and confusion and as always Susie's delight in the Christmas season was very much like that of the two boys. The house was handsomely decorated with Christmas green and there was a small but beautifully proportioned and elaborately decorated tree. Apparently Santa Claus had brought the boys everything their hearts had hungered for, because if there was the faintest cloud of disappointment in their bliss it was not apparent to their father. Susie had been awed and a little frightened by her very first fur coat. Not lordly mink by any means, but a far more modest dyed squirrel that had cost a little over three hundred dollars but could not have pleased her more if it had cost ten times as much.

She had slipped it on over her rumpled house dress and faced the mirror and winced.

"Trouble about anything so gorgeous," she told him frankly, "is that it's going to take a lot of living-up-to! My hair—maybe I should get a permanent. And perhaps one of those 'rinses that are not a dye, but bring out the hidden loveliness of your hair' like they are always yapping about on the radio. Only anything that could bring out the 'hidden beauty' of hair-colored hair like mine would have to go pretty deep, don't you think?"

She was completely in earnest, frowning as she studied her image, and Steve laughed at her and caught her close in his arms, and rubbed his cheek against her hair.

"You take one step toward a beauty parlor to have

anything done to your hair, and you'll get the walloping of a lifetime," he promised. "I like you just exactly the way you are—I wouldn't change so much as a freckle!"

She relaxed happily in his arms and sighed.

"I do love you so much. I think you're the nicest husband I ever had!" she told him joyously. "I'd like to be beautiful—if you'd like me to be—but if you're satisfied with me as I am, then hooray for us!"

"Hooray for us is right!" he told her firmly.

She was silent for a moment, clinging to him. And then without lifting her face, she asked huskily, "Know what I'd like for next Christmas?"

Steve's eyebrows went up.

"My word, but you are the greedy one! Here it is barely nine o'clock on this Christmas and you're already plotting for the next one."

She hushed him quickly. "All I want is to spend it with you, my darling."

She raised her lips to his and they held each other in a long, full kiss. When Steve's desire became obvious and Susie's breath was coming hard, she moved her mouth away.

"With you," she added, "and the boys' Little Sister. I want to have her by then."

Steve smiled at her; they kissed again, this time longer and more ardently than before.

Holding her body tightly against his, Steve said, "Come, my darling wife."

Arms around each other's waist, the two walked slowly up the stairs to their bedroom.

10. Partner in Crime

THE PHONE RANG AGAIN IN STEVE'S office. He answered it.

"Dr. Prescott speaking."

"Steve? This is Laura."

"Yes, Laura. How are you?" He felt distinctly annoyed at hearing her voice.

"This isn't a social call, Steve. I need your help professionally. It's important. You won't let me down, will you?"

He wanted to refuse, he wanted to tell her to call some other doctor, that it was impossible for him to do anything for her now, that he was busy.

"What's wrong, Laura?"

"It's not for me, Steve. It's for my patient."

"What seems to be the trouble?"

"Oh, Steve, that's why I need you. You'll see when you get here. Please?"

"Laura, I'm terribly busy today. Wouldn't another doctor do as well?"

"You know that I don't trust anyone as much as I do you. My patient needs a really good doctor. Please, Steve, —this one time."

"All right," he said. "Where are you and how do I get there?"

Laura gave him lengthy and involved instructions; each additional direction irritated him more.

"It begins to sound like a labyrinth," he commented.

"Oh, Steve, please. I promise you, this is purely professional. And I'll never bother you again."

"See you as soon as I can get there," he said.

"Thanks, Steve."

They hung up.

He postponed the remaining appointments on his calendar, called Susie and explained. He had to go out on another emergency, he said, and he had no idea when he would get back. She understood, as always, and her sweetness made Steve feel unaccountably guilty—had she known he was going to see Laura Weston, professionally or otherwise, she would not have been so trusting.

He drove carefully and thoughtfully, meticulously putting down any stirrings of lust. He would be aloof with Laura, treat the patient, and promptly return home.

He made each turn, following the complicated directions, and soon he saw the place Laura had described. It looked lonely and forlorn, at least a mile from the nearest neighbor, sitting on a hill top, shabby and shivering beneath the lash of the wind.

As he stopped the car and got out, the door opened, revealing an oblong of amber light. He saw someone standing there. It was Laura. As he went up the steps and along the narrow, sagging verandah she came anxiously to meet him.

"Steve, it's wonderful of you to come out on a night like this," her voice was warm and faintly husky as she laid a hand on his arm and drew him into the house. "But then, I knew you would."

Steve nodded, dropping his overcoat and hat, and standing close to the small, cheerful fire he warmed his hands as he demanded details. Laura gave them swiftly and efficiently, every inch the perfect nurse.

It was a maternity case, which did not surprise him since much of his practice was obstetrics though he did not specialize in it. And according to Laura's swift recital, the woman was in a bad way.

Steve shot a stern glance at Laura, but held back the words on his lips and said curtly, "I'll have a look at her."

"Yes, Doctor," said Laura meekly and led the way down the hall. She opened a door to a room where a woman lay in a high, narrow hospital bed, her face blue with anguish, her hands clenched so tightly that the knuckles were small white mounds above the delicate skin.

The room was neat, clean, bare, cheerless. So much his eyes took in before he reached the side of the bed and began his swift examination. The woman seemed so racked with pain that she was scarcely conscious of him, and when he had finished his examination he straightened and gave her the only sedative he dared, in her condition, to administer. He returned to the small living room, where a moment later Laura joined him.

"All right," he said curtly. "Who is she?"

"She gave me her name as Ann Smith," said Laura quietly.

Steve shot her a startled glance, frowning.

"You don't know her name? Her real name?" he demanded.

She spread her hands in a graceful gesture characteristic of her and said gently, "My patients pay very well for— anonymity. I could not afford to ask too many questions, with the fees they pay."

Steve stood quite still, staring at her and Laura smiled faintly, mockingly, a bitter look in her eyes.

"Yes, Doctor," she drawled deliberately. "This is one of those wicked, sinful, unlicensed maternity homes you loathe! Are you just terribly shocked?"

"I am. To find a nurse of your capabilities—!"

She shrugged mockingly.

"Oh, well, even a nurse of my capabilities must have a job—and you made it rather difficult for me to get another job, discharging me so abruptly without notice; Dr. Hurst's gossip about my friendship for poor Anna didn't help any. So—one does what one must," she assured him bitingly, bitterly derisive.

Steve was unable to answer, but his expression seemed to delight her.

"After all, Doctor, you are such a great humanitarian. Since you feel that the poorest and humblest, the most poverty-stricken regardless of race, creed or color, should have the best medical attention possible, don't you think poor unfortunates like 'Ann Smith' are entitled to decent treatment from an accredited physician?" she purred malevolently.

"I think 'poor unfortunates' like this 'Ann Smith' should be in hospitals, properly cared for, yes—by all means. I'll call an ambulance—" Steve reached for the telephone on the desk, but Laura laughed and took it from him and put it down again.

"Oh, no, you won't, darling—you'll look after her here, yourself," she told him. "We are very well equipped—come and see."

And Steve found himself, dazed and incredulous, following her down the small hall and into a tiny, but surprisingly well-equipped delivery room; adjoining it there was a small nursery with whose appointments he could find no fault. Across the hall there were two more bedrooms, each with three narrow beds crowded into it. Apparently there was only one private room and Ann Smith occupied it.

Puzzled, he assured himself that the place was amazingly well appointed, and then he turned sharply to Laura. She had lit a cigarette and was leaning against the door, watching him, acrid amusement washing out much of the loveliness of her blue eyes.

"Who operates this place?" he demanded sharply.

Laura tipped ash delicately from her cigarette into a cheap glass tray on the white-painted bureau beside her, and said sweetly, "I do—with the assistance of Anna, of course."

Steve was rocked back on his heels; despite his efforts to conceal the fact, he knew that she realized it. She laughed again and turned away, leading the way back to the living room. There she dropped into a chair, smiling up at him, triumphant, wickedly enjoying his shocked amazement.

She snuffed out her cigarette and relaxed in the chair

"Poor Anna," she drawled. "She's wonderful in obstetrics as long as I can keep her sober, and off the needle. But the moment I take my eye off her—zingo! She's off again. I had to send her away for a 'cure' and I hadn't planned to accept any more patients until she returned. But when 'Ann Smith' came along, offering two thousand dollars for good care and complete discretion—well, after all, two grand is an awful lot of money!"

Steve had listened in shocked, disgusted silence and when she finished he said harshly, "Of course you know that I shall have to report this place—and you—to the proper authorities!"

Her smile was evil, taunting, brimming with ugliness.

"Oh, I don't think you'll do that, darling," she said pleasantly. "I'm not a bit worried about your squealing—even with that Sir Galahad complex you seem to have been born with."

"You know how any decent doctor with an ordinary set of ethics loathes these places—"

"Professional jealousy?" she wondered amiably.

"You know that I have to report it."

Her smile was like a hand laid on his lips silencing him.

"You won't report me, darling, nor the location of this place," she told him, superbly sure of what she was saying. "If you are sensible, you will see that there are always going to be women like 'Ann Smith' who get themselves into jams and who need—and deserve—and can well afford to pay for—the best of medical services, but who dare not risk discovery of their little 'secret' by going to a hospital, or to a physician like you. So they fall into the hands of—butchers was the word you used, I believe. And their bodies are wrecked, their lives ruined—do you think that fair?"

"Just what are you getting at?"

"Why, I thought I had made it very plain, darling—I'm offering you a half-interest in a gold mine that ought to net us both about ten times what you are earning now, and with half the amount of work."

Steve gasped, choking down an oath, at the sheer audacity of that, his eyes blazing with healthy, quite honest fury.

"You're asking me to get mixed up in this—this—evil-smelling racket?" he demanded when he could trust himself to speak.

"I'm telling you that you are already mixed up in it, angel," she told him sweetly. "Remember Louise?"

"Your sister?"

"She wasn't my sister. You were a fool to have believed that for so much as a minute!" Her voice was touched with derision. "She was a patient from here—one of Anna's—well, less careful jobs. Poor Anna had managed to get herself a snootful of cocaine and wasn't—well, at her best when Louise's baby decided to be born."

Laura's face darkened with angry memory.

"She botched things so miserably the baby died—and I had arrangements made for it to be adopted by some very nice people who could easily afford a thousand dollars for the privilege," she finished, almost as though she had forgotten his presence.

Steve drew a deep, tortured breath and was silent for a long moment before he could trust his voice.

"So it is not only an unlicensed, illegal nursing home—it's also a black market in babies! You're heading for a rap, Laura. I find it hard to believe you could be mixed up in anything so foul—" his voice was thick and harsh with disgust.

Laura raised her eyebrows airily and her smile was soft and warm.

"You're mixed up in it too, darling. Louise is prepared to go on the witness stand at your trial and swear that you performed an illegal operation on her, from which she almost died," she told him gently.

Steve felt as though he had been kicked in the stomach. He could only look at Laura, wondering how he could have thought her beautiful. It sickened him to think that with her he had once enjoyed an hour of forbidden rapture.

Laura's color rose slightly at the loathing in his eyes. She sat up, stiffening, her head held arrogantly high, her eyes cold as the wind that rattled the shutters.

"So you see, Steve, you might just as well play along nicely, and take your half of the profits. I can assure you that the amount the place takes in, both from looking after the mothers and from the adoption part, would stagger you," she told him coldly. "Anna won't be coming back; I've decided that she's too dangerous to have around. But you and I, Steve—what a team we'll make!"

There was a breathless eagerness in her voice. She rushed on.

"And think what you could do for your family, Steve! That cheap, ridiculous fur coat you gave Susie—it could be a mink! The house could be done over—better still, you could move into something really nice, out in the Pace's Ferry Road section—the children's future would be assured—"

"And their father could confidently expect that at any minute the long and very heavy arm of the law would fall on him and drag him off to a ten-to-twenty year rap in the penitentiary. Thanks, Laura—that's not for me!" he told her savagely and caught up his hat and coat.

"So you are determined to turn me in? Throw me to the wolves?" she asked quietly, and there was not the faintest touch of disturbance in her voice. She seemed no more than idly amused.

"Much as I hate to do it, Laura—you know I have to," he told her.

"Knowing that the minute I'm arrested, I'll implicate you, with Louise to swear that it was you who did the illegal surgery? That's a pretty ugly charge, darling. You know what it would mean to Susie and the boys, don't you? And you're not fool enough to think you could beat the rap—with Louise identifying you positively."

"Which would mean her own reputation would be ruined in the process—"

Laura tipped back her pretty head and laughed as though that were the best joke in the world.

"Louise's reputation? Darling, she lost that when she was about fourteen! Louise is a cheap little floozie who was fool enough to let herself get pregnant, because she thought that way she could force her current boy friend to marry her. But he enlisted in the army and was deep in Korea before she even knew that he wasn't just away on one of his semi-annual business trips. She was furious, of course, because her condition, as soon as it became obvious, cut down her earning capacity. She came to me, and I had an application for a healthy boy-baby, and I took her in. Then Anna muffed the delivery and the baby died. And Louise damned near did, too. I simply can't afford to lose babies that way. The market is booming—"

Steve spoke a single word, an unprintable word that made Laura stop speaking. The color went out of her face and her eyes grew diamond-bright and as cold.

"Nevertheless, whatever I am, Steve—and I deny nothing!—you are going to help me. Or Louise and I will ruin you for all time to come!" she told him. "As a matter of fact, much as I'd like to have you as my partner, and knowing how much money we could drag down, I think I am a sufficiently poor business woman to hope that you do try to turn me in. It would be real fun for me to get on the witness stand and allow myself, under cross-examination, to admit with tearful reluctance that the reason I left your employ so precipitately was because I had discovered that you were performing illegal operations and my high ethics as a nurse would not permit me to countenance such horrible deeds."

He had been listening to her incredulously. His face had whitened until his jaw was tight and hard, but not once did he try to interrupt. There was a taut silence when she had finished, and then she made a small gesture with one soft, white hand.

"And then, too," she said slowly, "I think I'd get a real kick out of telling Susie about our stolen night together. That homely pudding-face of hers ought to be something to watch—"

Before he could check his fury, his hand had gone out and he had slapped her hard across the cheek.

"You—" The filthy epithet thickened his voice.

Laura looked up at him and now all pretense of mockery was gone.

"Let's stop slashing at each other with insults, Steve, and get right down to brass tacks, shall we? Ann Smith is past the age for easy child-bearing; she has laced herself into a tight corset in the hope of concealing her condition as long as she could, and you and I both know how much more dangerous that makes her condition. Only a thoroughly competent and able man who has had your experience in obstetrics can hope to save her—and the baby. And you're going to do it, no matter what I have to do to force you!"

He was shaken in spite of himself, but he managed, "I suppose you have a fine home all fixed up for the baby —at a handsome fee."

"Believe it or not, Ann intends to keep the baby—"

"Yet she risks her life—and the life of the baby—by sneaking into a place like this in order to keep her secret?"

"She will adopt the baby, of course, on a trip out west or down to Florida. She is a wealthy woman of a prominent, socially distinguished family. She wants the baby and she can give it every advantage, once it is safely born," she told him sharply.

Suddenly she was on her feet, all warmth and gentleness, coaxing, pleading.

"Steve, forget for a moment that you had yourself that night with me—and remember only that you are a doctor and that this woman needs you as few of your patients have ever needed you. Be big enough, just once in your life, Steve, if you never are again, to do something fine and beautiful and real, even if it isn't exactly within the bounds of your narrow-minded, self-righteous profession. Give her a break, Steve. She's been through hell. She deserves the best you can give her. Forget about me and Susie and everything but 'Ann Smith' and her child. It has a right to live, Steve; it didn't ask to be born into this kind of a mess, but it has a right to come into the world safely, protected by all the skill you can exert—please, Steve!"

Grimly, after a moment, he nodded, and went back to the room where Ann Smith had gained a brief respite from the agonized suffering, and he stood for a moment looking down at her face, blue-white, wet with the cold sweat of her anguish. She looked delicately bred, a woman of culture and refinement. His heart was wrung with angry pity. You'd expect a woman of this sort to have enough intelligence to keep herself free from such a mess—but sex is no respecter of persons, as he had good cause to know. And when at last he left the cottage, it was with the promise that he would return when Laura called to tell him that the ordeal of labor had begun. Meanwhile, there were small things that her training and her professional skill could provide for the woman's temporary ease.

Laura stood beside the window in the intense darkness of the hour just before dawn, and saw the lights of Steve's car fade away beyond the curve in the road. And when she dropped the curtain and turned back into the room, her lovely face was white, and there was a look of uneasiness very close to panic in her eyes.

11. False Witness

LAURA LOOKED IN ON THE so-called Ann in the morning, saw that she seemed to be sleeping quietly, and with a huge sigh of relief, went along to the bathroom where she took a shower. She had had no sleep for twenty-four hours and she was exhausted. She had no intention of going to sleep when she dropped down across one of the beds in a back room. But exhaustion, the relaxing of her too-taut nerves by the warm shower, conspired against her. She fell asleep almost instantly.

When she awoke, the late, watery sunshine of mid-afternoon was spilling through the windows and she sprang up, alert and worried. Wearing nothing but her terry towel bathrobe and heelless scuffs, she hurried in to Ann—and her heart rose smotheringly in her breast. For a moment she swayed and had to cling to the door frame to keep from falling. Because she had seen death too often in her professional career to have the slightest doubt, even from where she stood, that Ann was dead.

She gave a small, low moan deep in her throat. She fought down the panic within her and forced herself to go to the bed. She stood looking down at the calm white face with its bluish shadows. Without hope, she touched the already cool wrists, laid her hand across the full white breast beneath which there was no throb of life.

The woman was dead!

Once more the black edge of panic touched her; but again she fought it down. From the very first moment when she and Dr. Harmon had set out on this devious, danger-ous business, she had realized quite coldly that some day this could happen, and had prepared herself for it.

She moved swiftly, purposefully.

69

She dressed in a nondescript dark suit, tied a scarf over her hair that concealed every shining strand. Without make-up, she looked older and her present pallor added to her plainness. There were glasses, too, black-rimmed, cheap, as nondescript as her suit.

Without a backward glance at the woman, she hurried out into the bitter cold of the morning, shivering in the thin suit, her large handbag held tightly beneath her arm. There was a shabby, mud-stained coupe in the garage and she got into it, swearing savagely as the motor, cold now, whirred for a moment or two before it caught. And then she backed the car into the road and turned it towards town.

She chose a parking lot near a neighborhood shopping center, where the car was lost amid a welter of inexpensive cars whose housewife drivers were shopping in the neighborhood.

She took a bus into the heart of town, and alighted in front of a huge department store. Then she hurried a block north to the railroad station. She mixed with the group of a dozen or more who were in front of the ticket-window and bought a ticket to Savannah. A train would be leaving in fifteen minutes.

She waited five minutes and then she dialed Steve's office, and when she heard his voice, tired and impatient, she had no difficulty in throwing into her voice all the terror and the panic that had been dogging her for the last hour.

"Steve, you must come immediately—there isn't a moment to spare. She's—I'm terribly frightened, Steve—" her voice broke.

"I'll leave immediately," said Steve and his voice was harsh.

Laura permitted herself a very small smile, and watched the clock. She waited until only two minutes remained before train time, and the calls were already being made over the loudspeaker and people were beginning to move towards the stairs that led down to train level. And then she dropped another coin into the telephone, and dialed police headquarters.

When she heard the bored voice on the other end of the wire, she rushed into speech, keeping her voice high and slightly nasal, touched with excitement.

"Look," she said, "I kinda think you folks ought to know about some funny goin's on at a bungalow out on Lawson Road. All of us that live out along there have been wonderin' about things—I live two miles beyond and I been sellin' butter and eggs to 'em. Well, just now when I come to deliver their stuff, they wasn't nobody home but the door was unlocked and I jest went on in to the kitchen to put the stuff on the table—and they's a dead woman out there!"

"Who are you?" demanded the officer and his voice was no longer bored.

"My name's Smith—Mis' Ann Smith." Her mouth curved in an unlovely grin.

"You out there now?"

"I sure am—"

"O.K., wait there—we'll send somebody out—how do we get there?"

She gave him the directions, saw the gate about to close above the stairs to the train and slipped the receiver into place and went running across the station to the stairs, and down to where a porter was waiting to help her on the train. There was a smile of malicious pleasure on her lips as she settled herself breathlessly in her seat, still clutching the big, unfashionable but capacious bag close in her arms. . . .

Steve took advantage of his privilege as a doctor on an emergency call to make the trip as swiftly as he dared. Yet it seemed to him that he was merely crawling and that hours had elapsed since that frantic call from Laura.

He sprang from the car beside the shabby bungalow and ran across the drive and into the house. He stopped for an instant, because there was something curiously ominous about the utter silence of the place. Where was Laura?

He went swiftly to the room where "Ann Smith" lay— and, like Laura, he knew death when he saw it. He stood stock-still, feeling as though he had been bludgeoned. He had realized the night before that her condition was critical, but had hoped against hope that she would manage to cling to life. He went through all the motions of determining that she was really dead even though his first glimpse of her had told him that she was.

He was so dazed, so shaken by the reality of her death that he did not hear a car drive up, nor the steps of men crossing the narrow verandah. He turned his head as the outer door swung open and called out sharply, "Laura—is that you?"

And then the doorway was practically filled by a large, beefy-looking man whose "plain clothes" shrieked "cop" as loudly as did the familiar blue uniforms of the two men who stood behind him. They were staring into the room, looking swiftly from Steve to the still, blue-white corpse against the pillows, taking in the familiar black bag that proclaimed Steve's profession.

"What—?" Steve had to moisten his lips before he could go on with the idiotic question, "What are you doing here?"

"We had a call from a woman in the neighborhood who reported there was a dead woman here," said the big man, and came on into the room, looking at Steve curiously. "I suppose she called you, too. Or is the woman a patient of yours? Was, I mean—I take it she's dead."

"Oh, yes, she's dead," said Steve tautly. "I was called in to treat her last night. I knew she was in a bad way. But was unable to get her to a hospital—"

"Sure," nodded the big man, and flashed his credentials at Steve and said pleasantly, "I'm Jordan, Homicide."

"I'm Dr. Prescott," said Steve.

The two men who had loomed behind Jordan had faded quietly away and Steve heard them going through the house, and waited tensely. Where was Laura? The thought kept plucking at his mind, which was in such a turmoil now that he was not quite certain what he was saying.

"What was the patient's trouble?" asked Jordan, and then looked at the ungainly middle of the thin body and said awkwardly, "Maternity, eh, Doctor? Something went wrong?"

"I—yes," said Steve and forced himself to speak quietly, as nearly matter-of-fact as his mental turmoil would allow. "She was past the age for easy childbirth. She had tried to disguise her condition by lacing herself tightly, to a point where it became very dangerous. I don't think she has had medical attention—until recently—"

"Cards stacked against her, eh? Hell of a note—where's her husband?" asked Jordan almost innocently.

"I don't imagine she had one," Steve told him grimly.

"Oh, one of those, eh? Poor dame," said Jordan. To Steve it seemed obscene that they should stand here over this woman who had given her life to protect her pathetic secret, while they discussed that secret in the most brutal possible fashion.

One of the blue-uniformed men appeared unobtrusively in the doorway and cleared his throat.

"Like to show you something, Lieutenant," he said, obviously trying to conceal his rising excitement.

Jordan glanced at him, and then back at Steve and suddenly the friendly dark eyes had become hard and cold, as he nodded and went out of the room behind the uniformed officer.

Steve knew, of course, what they had found; the small, compact but amazingly efficient and well-equipped delivery room; the two rooms fitted up as wards; and God alone knew what else!

He went into the living room, having drawn the sheet neatly up over the cadaver's still face, and let himself down into the chair where last night Laura had sat, so composed, so savage, so sure that he would help her. Again the thought came, plaguing, worrying: Where was Laura?

He didn't know how long he had been there when Jordan came back, and stood looking at him, cold-eyed, grim.

"Better start talking, Doc," he said after a long moment of silent scrutiny.

Steve made a small gesture of defeat with the hand that held his cigarette.

"You've found the delivery room, of course, the nursery, the two wards—there's not much for me to do but admit the place is a private maternity home, is there?" he asked grimly.

"Private—and unlicensed," Jordan pointed out. "D'you know, Doc, I've got a hunch we've trapped one of the sources for that illegal adoption racket the newspapers like to call the black market in babies—you know that?"

Steve sat very still for a long moment, but realized that he dared not attempt to evade or deny what Jordan said.

"I'm afraid you have, Lieutenant."

"Afraid is the right word, Doc—afraid you're going to have to do a hell of a lot of talking before you're out of this," said Jordan grimly. "Who runs this joint? Or am I being stupid? Finding you here with the dead body of a patient sounds kind of like you might have more than a passing interest in it."

"I never entered this place in my life until last night," Steve told him, and saw disbelief in the man's eyes, but went doggedly on. "A former office nurse of mine called me at around midnight last night and said she was on a private-duty case. She said the patient had had a bad turn, and her own doctor was out of town. My former nurse put the matter so urgently, that I came out."

Jordan nodded, obviously not quite willing to accept so simple an explanation yet playing it cautiously.

"But you must have tumbled to what was going on, Doc. You couldn't have missed it. I've heard about you, Dr. Prescott. You do a lot of charity work—have a fine reputation. How come you didn't turn the joint in, the minute you saw the set-up?" he asked, polite but firm, and still obviously not quite sure whether he could accept Steve's explanation or not.

Steve hesitated a long time. Then he said harshly, "I'm afraid I can't answer that, at the moment."

"Can't talk until you have your mouthpiece on hand? That's your privilege, of course, Doc—but it doesn't look too good, for you!" Jordan pointed out grimly. "If you're on the level, then you ought to be just as anxious to

clean up these dumps as we are. We've had fine coopera-
tion from most of the doctors who come in contact with
this messy business."

Steve did not answer. When they found Laura—
where was Laura?

Another car had arrived and the door opened and
there was a murmur of voices and then the police-surgeon,
a man Steve had known for some time, came in.

"Hell, Prescott—you're not the fellow who's—"
Cooper, startled, broke off and glanced at Jordan.

Jordan gestured towards the room where "Ann Smith"
lay, and Cooper, puzzled and uneasy, went through the
door and silence fell upon Jordan and Steve.

It seemed to Steve, caught up in a dazed feeling that
this was all some sort of evil nightmare, that hours passed
before Cooper came back. He nodded to Jordan, glanced
at Steve still in angry bewilderment and went out.

Two white-coated men came in, passed into the room
where "Ann Smith" lay, carrying a wicker basket between
them. When they, too, had gone, a uniformed officer
came to Jordan, bent low and whispered in his ear. Jordan
nodded and the man went away.

"This former office-nurse of yours, Doc, that you say
runs this place—any idea where she might be found?"
he asked almost casually. "She doesn't seem to be around."

"Oh, but—she wouldn't leave—" Steve cut short the
startled protest at the look in Jordan's eyes.

"She seems to have done just that—like a bat out
of hell," said Jordan grimly. "Must have found the patient
dead, given you a ring and then, for good measure, called
us—"

"But I thought you said your call came from a woman
living in the neighborhood," Steve protested.

"Speaking from a pay station, somewhere, in a voice
that sounded faked—" Jordan stood up and shrugged into
his overcoat. "Any idea where she might go?"

"She has an apartment at the Towers," said Steve
reluctantly.

"Suppose we drop in on her, Doc," suggested Jordan

in a tone that for all its formality indicated it would be very wise indeed for Steve to agree.

Outside in the swift-gathering early dusk, beaten by a chill wind that had the bite of ice in it, Jordan spoke to the two uniformed men in the prowl-car and came over to Steve.

"You'd better drive, since it's your boat, Doc," he said as he got into the car. "The boys will follow."

Steve drove wordlessly, scarcely listening to Jordan's casually matter-of-fact conversation that had nothing to do with the black horror which had so suddenly erupted about Steve's head. When they reached the apartment house, Steve parked in the lot beside the building and he and Jordan walked together into the lobby. Out of the corner of his eye, Steve saw the prowl-car beside his own, and the two uniformed men station themselves where they could keep an eye on the entrance.

He and Jordan crossed the lobby to the elevator and Steve asked the operator, "Miss Weston in?"

The operator looked startled.

"Miss Weston moved out, Doctor—two-three weeks ago. Her apartment has been sub-let," he answered, surprised that Laura's employer would not know that.

Jordan eyed Steve for a long moment, his face hard, his eyes cold, and then he gestured to a seat beside a pot of growing plants and said curtly, "Suppose you wait here, Doc. I'll have words with the manager."

Steve sat down and for a moment covered his face with his hands. He was so desperately tired; his mind was so dazed that there was room in his conscious thoughts only for Susie and the boys. And his very insides went cold at the realization of what he had done to them.

He had no notion of how long Jordan had been gone, but at last he was coming back across the lobby, moving with long, purposeful strides, and as he stood above Steve, his hands sunk deeply into his pockets, his eyes were grim.

"The Weston gal sub-let her apartment almost a month ago and sent her belongings to storage," he announced. "Said she had a job out of town and would send for the things later. Still want to tell me she was running that joint out there?"

"So far as I know—" Steve began stiffly, but the look in Jordan's eyes silenced him and his jaw grew hard and taut.

"Let's take a little ride downtown, Doc. A couple of fellows at Headquarters would like to hear your story," suggested Jordan dryly. He turned and strode across the lobby and out into the bitter night, Steve meekly following.

At Headquarters, Steve told his story evenly, quietly, knowing there was nothing else to be done. And when he had finished, the man from the District Attorney's office, seated at the desk beside the Captain of the Homicide Squad, asked questions. Steve answered them and saw the colorless secretary take down his answers in black and white, and knew that his professional career was doomed. Laura had vanished. He was left holding the bag and that was that.

When the ordeal was over, the man from the District Attorney's office consulted with the Captain of the Homicide Squad for a moment in low tones, and then turned to Steve.

"That will be all for now, Dr. Prescott," he said formally.

Steve was startled.

"You are not placing me under arrest?" he asked.

"Not at the moment," said the attorney cautiously. "We are releasing you under your own recognizance. Naturally, we will expect you to hold yourself in readiness to—er— render any possible assistance in clearing things up and locating this—former nurse. I don't think there is any danger of your leaving town suddenly, is there, Dr. Prescott?"

"Hardly," said Steve through his teeth and could not meet the eyes of these men who were tacitly certain that he had been mixed up in what was surely one of the foulest businesses in which any doctor could have a hand. He walked out, forcing himself to hold his head erect despite the inclination to slink out like a kicked cur with its tail between its legs.

12. The Fall Guy

HE DID NOT GO HOME UNTIL HE was quite sure that the boys had been put to bed. Facing Susie was the hardest thing he had ever had to do in his life. He had sat for hours in his office, the door locked, the lights out, his numbed mind trying to pull itself together to face all the ugly consequences that were like an evil cloud about him. And all of it had sprung from an hour of illicit pleasure in Laura Weston's bed! That had been the first tentacle of the web she had woven so closely, so snugly about him. That woman she had presented as her sister; then the offer of her body and his falling for the lure, baited with the oldest, surest bait in the world—forbidden sex!

He drove home at last and put the car in the garage. There were lights in the living room but the bedrooms and kitchen showed only darkness. Even after he had garaged the car and switched off the motor, he sat for a little before he could gather the courage to go into the house. When he went up the steps of the back entrance, lights flashed in the kitchen, and the door swung open and Susie stood there, waiting for him.

Susie, so sweet and good, so adoring—so unquestioning in her loyalty—suddenly he had caught her close in his arms, because he could not endure the radiance in her loving face.

"Darling, you're scandalously late," she protested lovingly. "I do hope you had a good hot dinner—or am I being silly to think you'd remember anything like food when a patient needs you?"

For a moment he held her close, resting his worn and weary spirit in the blessedness of her unquestioning faith and adoration. And Susie clung to him radiantly, and stood on tiptoe to kiss him, and said eagerly, "I'll get you something to eat—"

"No, darling, I couldn't eat. I'm not hungry. I have—something—pretty terrible to tell you," said Steve knowing that the moment could not be put off; knowing that it must be now and here; because he could not be sure of what moment a warrant would be sworn out for his arrest. Especially if they did not find Laura. . . .

"Honey, what is it? Steve darling—nothing can be so terrible while we have each other. Don't look like that!" she cried out wildly as she saw his face clearly for the first time since he had come into the kitchen.

"Susie, what is the very worst thing you can possibly think could happen to us?" It was not the question he had meant to ask; it had slipped out of his tormented mind.

"That you'd stop loving me," she told him instantly.

"Then you've nothing to worry about because I'll never stop loving you as long as I live. But you might easily stop loving me when I have finished what I have to say," he said humbly.

"And pigs might fly, and prices might come down and the Russians might get tired of making war—only I don't think it's very likely, do you?" said Susie sturdily, and drew him into the living room and pushed him down into his favorite chair. She perched on his knee, an arm about his shoulder.

"Poor lamb!" she crooned as though he had been Bill with a bumped head or a cut finger, and for a moment he relaxed in the blessed warmth of her love. But at last he knew that he could not delay any longer, and so he looked at her, forcing a grimace that was a very unsuccessful smile.

"Well, here goes," he said. Beginning with the night Laura had called to ask him to see her "sister," Steve told Susie the whole ugly story, sparing himself nothing. As he spoke, he felt her arm relax about his shoulder and by the time he had finished she had gone to perch on the edge of a chair across from him, and his heart quailed at the knowledge that she could no longer endure the touch of him.

She waited, her face growing whiter and whiter, until the gay little parade of freckles across her pert nose stood out against that pallor. Her eyes had the sick, frightened look he had seen in the eyes of small animals caught in cruel, steel-jawed traps.

He finished at last and leaned back, exhausted. He knew that she could not possibly forgive him, that as soon as her trembling knees could support her, she would rise and walk up the stairs and out of his life, taking with her the two small boys that he loved only a little less than he loved her.

He waited for her to speak. And he would not wait before the bar of justice, which he felt sure he would eventually reach, with more anxiety, more bitter, sickening suspense than he waited for the verdict from this taut, white-faced woman.

"And so you were—her lover," she said at last in a small, strangled voice and it was obvious that she had for the moment brushed all the rest of his ugly story from her mind. "When, Steve?"

He told her, and he saw her eyes grow intent for a moment before she drew a small, shaken sigh.

"Before we started Little Sister," she breathed at last and there was a note of relief in her voice that made him look at her sharply. And Susie nodded, answering the question before he could put it into words, "Oh, yes, we've started—Little Sister. I've known it for two or three days. I was planning a sort of special announcement party—" her voice broke and for a moment her face was hidden in her hands.

"Susie—darling, darling Susie—" his voice was thick and broken.

She flung up her head and looked at him, her face streaked with tears, her eyes holding his.

"I—just have to know—one thing," she told him huskily.

"I had nothing to do with the nursing home, nor the babies—" he began swiftly, but her little almost contemptuous gesture silenced him.

"Oh, of course, I know that!" she dismissed it as of the

very smallest importance. "What I have to know is—did you enjoy it?"

His illicit hour of passion with Laura had dropped out of his mind, because it seemed so absurdly unimportant compared to the other charges which could be leveled against him. For a moment, he was almost puzzled by her question.

"Enjoy it?" he repeated stupidly.

Her face was twisted with a convulsive pain, and her tongue touched her dry, pallid lips before she could get the words out to answer him.

"Did you enjoy—sleeping with Laura?" she seemed to spit the words out. "Though that's a silly way to express it. I'm sure you didn't do any sleeping. But was it fun, making love to her?"

There was such bitter pain, such savage jealousy in her voice, that it was almost weirdly funny, Steve told himself, badly shaken.

"If you lie to me, Steve, I'll never forgive you. Was it fun? Did you—like it?" her small, taut voice flung the words at him like tiny, savage blows.

Steve said thinly, "I'm a man, Susie. She's—a beautiful and alluring woman—"

Susie stood up, trembling so that she put out her hand and clung to the back of her chair, facing him with her small face so taut that it could have been carved of stone.

"And being a man, you loved it. You must have found me very inadequate after her—" she spat at him.

"Susie, you are my wife—I adore you—"

"So much that you get a terrific kick out of loving another woman any time she takes 'em off for you! And I bet a lot of them do!" she flung at him.

The words would have been merely mildly vulgar, to be dismissed without thought; coming from Susie, with her honest, straightforward clean young mind they were downright shocking.

"Susie dearest—you know that isn't true," Steve told her swiftly. "I have never touched another woman since the day I met you. Except Laura. And the minute it was over I hated her."

"I don't believe you—I don't believe you—" Susie's wail was like that of a grief-stricken child as she turned blindly towards the stairs. So blindly that before she had gone three steps she stumbled, and Steve caught her and held her close.

For a moment she fought him furiously, hysteria clogging her throat, her small clenched fists beating against his breast. But the fight lasted not more than a moment and then her arms slid about him and she hid her face against him and wept out her grief and her shock against his shoulder.

Steve drew her down into his lap and cradled her close against him, and let her tears flow to the finish. And at last when she had regained some measure of control and had wiped her eyes and blown her nose as vigorously as Bill might have done, she looked up at him, white and worn, with the small smile he so dearly loved trembling about her mouth.

"What happens next?" she asked huskily.

Steve hesitated but he owed her nothing less than the truth.

"I'm afraid it's going to be pretty bad," he admitted humbly. "Unless Laura is found—and can be persuaded to tell the truth."

"She won't be found," said Susie with savage emphasis. "So just don't count on it. What happens without her?"

"I don't quite know," he admitted honestly. "The fact that I was found, alone, with 'Ann Smith'—that the place was unlicensed, secretive—we might as well face it. One to five years in prison is the best I can hope for."

He felt her small body go rigid with shock, and her face that could go no paler, stiffened incredulously. She was unwilling to believe him.

"Prison?" she gasped. "You? Oh, my darling—no!"

His arms held her closely and his face was gray and damp with sweat.

"In which case," he went on harshly, "I will, of course, be dropped from the medical list, my license revoked. I will be denied the privilege of practicing my profession anywhere in the country."

She was so shocked, so appalled that words were denied her, and after a moment Steve went on grimly, "If—the worst happens, you and the boys will be provided for. Sell the place here; I might be able to dispose of my practice for a few hundreds—that will be all it's worth when this is over. You can go down to your father's farm and—well, I'm afraid that's it."

"But, Steve—surely nobody can believe that you had anything to do with such a loathsome business—not you, Steve. After all, you are not a stranger here. Surely people at the hospital—your patients—other doctors—"

"Most of whom would not even raise a finger in my defense, unless Laura can be found—" Steve told her grimly. "After all, 'Ann Smith' is dead—and I attended her—and was found beside her in the house—alone with her. Laura had been gone from the apartment for almost a month, claiming she was going North to work; there is only my own unsupported word that Laura was ever mixed up in the business at all—so—you see?"

"I see," said Susie huskily and for a moment they were both silent, appalled by the blackness all about them. "I see that you're in a terrible jam, and we've got to do something pretty smart to prove you are innocent—"

"Strictly speaking, Susie darling, I'm not," he reminded her. "I did attend the girl, Louise; I also attended 'Ann Smith.' There was ample time after I left the place last night for me to report it to the authorities, as any reputable physician would have done."

"Don't you dare indicate that you are not a reputable physician," she flashed hotly. "I'll scratch the eyes out of anybody who dares suggest it—" her voice died, and she sat up and looked at him curiously. "Why didn't you report it last night, darling?"

"Because Laura threatened, if I did, to take the witness stand and swear that she and I had been—lovers—" he admitted quite honestly. "I couldn't let her do that."

Her eyes were warm and tender and she bent her head and kissed him warmly.

"No, of course you couldn't, because of the boys—"

"Because I was fool enough to think I could keep *you*

from knowing—" he told her huskily, and held her close.

After a moment, her cheek pressed hard against his, she spoke soothingly as she would have spoken to one of the children.

"Don't you worry, darling," she said softly. "We'll see it through together and it won't be so bad—you wait and see."

And despite his deep conviction that it was going to be very bad indeed he allowed himself for a blessed moment to rest in the secure knowledge of her love. But the bitterness of realizing how little he deserved that unquestioning devotion tore at his heart.

13. Post Mortem

THE MORNING PAPERS CARRIED THE story, of course. Cautious, insinuating, rather than bold. Dr. Steven Prescott's name was given considerable publicity, but as yet there was nothing definitely known against him, save that he had been found with the dead woman—whom the papers, of course, were calling "the mystery woman"—and that she had died in childbirth. Certainly it was not the kind of publicity that aids a reputable doctor's career and Steve went to his office, tight-lipped and braced for any unpleasant eventuality.

Jane Middleton watched him anxiously as he took off his overcoat and hung it up, and when he had seated himself behind his desk, she put her uneasiness into awkward words.

"I saw the papers this morning, Dr. Prescott," she said formally.

"You could scarcely miss them, nurse."

"It's a terrible story, Dr. Prescott, but of course I know you are not guilty of anything—well, of anything unbecoming to a man of your profession."

"Thanks, nurse. That's very kind of you," said Steve.

She hesitated and then she turned to the door, but with her hand on the door-knob his voice stopped her.

"If you'd like to—resign your position, nurse—"

She turned swiftly and her plain, kind middle-aged face was flushed.

"Unless you'd like me to," she told him evenly, "I'll stick."

"Thanks. We'll leave it at that then."

She nodded and went out.

There were three cancellations of appointments that morning: maternity cases, Steve noticed and his mouth was a thin, wry line. Still you couldn't blame women who were approaching such an ordeal for wishing to be sure the attending physician was a man of the highest and most unimpeachable integrity. He made his usual rounds, and at the hospital he was aware of covert glances, of voices that dropped into guilty silence as he came in sight; but it was, of course, only what he had braced himself to face, though there was great bitterness within him.

When he came back to the office for his three-to-five o'clock appointments, Jordan was waiting for him. Steve merely nodded and held the door of his private office open for him, while the two or three patients who waited watched them curiously.

"Got some news for you, Doc, that won't be in the papers until in the morning," said Jordan casually as he seated himself in the patient's chair. "The 'mystery woman' has been identified and the body claimed."

"Oh?" said Steve and waited tautly.

"Name's Claire Lafferty—that name mean anything to you?"

"I'm afraid not."

"Very prominent family, very wealthy—the backbone of a small town in the southern part of the state," Jordan told him. "The Laffertys lived there for generations. Own the pulp mill, textile factory, the bank—just about the whole works. Claire was the spinster head of the family."

"Spinster?" Steve repeated.

Jordan grinned wryly.

"One of those," he agreed. "Never cared for men; never had a beau; seemed wrapped up in looking after the younger members of the family, all married now and absorbed in one or another of the family's enterprises. Claire lived alone in the old family home—alone except for the usual servants, that is. Nobody ever saw her out with a man, nobody would have believed that she could get herself into a mess like this."

"That explains her efforts to conceal her condition, of course," said Steve slowly.

"Sure," said Jordan. "One of her nephews very reluctantly admitted that about a year ago she hired a chauffeur—a young, good-looking fellow who had worked at a local filling station."

"The family, then, believes that she fell for the chauffeur?"

"It's the only way they can explain her being pregnant," said Jordan.

"Where is the chauffeur?"

"In the army—he was drafted and the draft board recalls that she made quite a pitch to get him deferred but they stood up against her." Jordan shrugged and seemed to feel the subject had been exhausted. "We got an order this morning and searched the Weston woman's belongings in storage. There were no records of any kind. That strike you as odd?"

"Under the circumstances, yes. She could not possibly have conducted that place without keeping some kind of records," said Steve.

"That's what we thought," said Jordan and there was an emphasis in his tone that Steve did not care for. "You wouldn't have any idea where she would keep such records?"

Steve's jaw hardened.

"Since I first knew of the existence of the place night before last, I'm afraid not," he said.

Jordan nodded, his eyes sharp and intent.

"Cooper estimated the woman had been dead at least three hours when he got there," he went on slowly. "Of course, that would have given the Weston woman ample time to burn whatever records she had. Think so?"

"I think it's quite likely," Steve had to admit.

Jordan sat smoking silently for a moment, eyeing Steve thoughtfully.

"We have no way of knowing how long the place had been operating," he pointed out. "Nor how many patients had been there. Nor whether they were patients who wanted—illegal operations—or adoption homes for the kids."

Steve said grimly, "Laura told me that the children were

placed for adoption at sizable fees. 'Ann Smith' intended
to adopt her own, it seems."

Jordan nodded, his eyes narrowing a little.

"Then without the records, we're up a stump," he said
grimly. "For nobody who 'buys' a baby on the 'black
market' is going to come forward and give evidence. If
the babies were taken over the state line, then that makes
it a federal offense and the F.B.I. comes into the case. If
the babies were kept within the state—which I think is
damned unlikely—then it's our pigeon. What do you think,
Doc?"

"I think," said Steve grimly, "that we'll never know until
you find Laura."

Jordan nodded.

"Shouldn't be too hard to find a good-looker like her,"
he said casually, but the look in his eyes was anything but
casual. "We have a very good description of her. No picture, unfortunately. Seems she was sort of allergic to
photographers. We found her car, though."

Startled, Steve stiffened.

Jordan nodded.

"Parked in a super-market's parking lot in a neighborhood not far from the apartment," said Jordan. "Em-
ployees noticed it last night at closing time, when nobody
came to remove it. It was still there this morning, so we
hauled it in. Gave it a going-over—no dice. But it's her
car. So she didn't skip out driving her own car. That
leaves us the bus stations, the railroad stations, and the
airport. Any idea what direction she would follow?"

"Not the slightest," said Steve, and added reluctantly,
"I have no idea whether it was the truth or not, but she
told me that she and Dr. Anna Harmon were running the
place between them, but that Harmon was on dope and
liquor pretty heavily and had had to be 'sent away' for a
cure."

Jordan nodded.

"We checked that," he explained. "There is no trace of
Harmon—though, of course, we have only checked the
known and reputable sanitariums in the immediate neigh-

borhood. We are checking farther and farther—but d'you know something, Doc? I'm beginning to wonder if the 'cure' Harmon was given wasn't a—permanent one."

Steve sat perfectly still for a moment, shocked, appalled by the implication of Jordan's statement.

"You think Harmon is—dead?" he asked at last.

"Don't you?" demanded Jordan almost sharply.

Steve's face was gray with shock.

"But—surely—she could not have disposed of a body!"

Jordan said grimly, "She was a registered nurse, you know. And must have learned quite a bit from this Harmon—" he let the sentence trail off. "We are having the grounds around that joint out there dug up—the cellar and all the rest of it. You never can tell, we might turn something up."

Steve was sick at the evil thing that loomed ahead. He could not quite accept the picture of Laura as a steel-nerved murderess, coldly disposing of the body of her friend—yet. . . . He shivered.

Jordan stood up, crushing out his cigarette in the ashtray on the desk, and said casually, "Be seein' you around, Doc."

Steve watched the door close behind the other and sat for a long moment, making a terrific effort to pull himself together before he signalled Jane Middleton to bring in the next patient. . . .

Steve was arrested the following morning. He was at breakfast with Susie and the boys when the men arrived; sensing their intention, he met them in the living room, with the door to the dining room closed against the children's voices—and ears.

"We have a warrant for your arrest, Dr. Prescott," said one of the men quietly, and displayed his badge. "Better pack a few things."

Steve nodded and found Susie beside him, white-faced but holding herself erect, her head high.

"Steve?" she asked unsteadily, her voice filled with alarm.

"Yes, darling. Keep your chin up—we'll fight it through," said Steve and turned towards the stairs.

One of the arresting officers moved behind him. Steve shot him a swift, angry glance. The man only smiled faintly and made a slight gesture that indicated he was merely doing his job, and followed Steve up the stairs.

Susie turned belligerently on the remaining man who looked uncomfortable before her blazing anger.

"This is the silliest, wickedest thing in the world," she flashed. "My husband is completely innocent. He's—he's —wonderful! He couldn't possibly be mixed up in anything foul—"

"He'll be held as a material witness, Mrs. Prescott. There won't be any formal charges filed against him—at least not right away," the man tried to soothe her awkwardly.

"But even being arrested, held as a material witness— why, that's awful for a man in his profession!" Susie's voice stumbled and broke, and she set her teeth hard in her lower lip.

"Believe me, Mrs. Prescott, I hate to do it—"

Steve and the other man came down the stairs, and Susie's heart twisted to see the bag Steve carried. Not the small bag that was a symbol of his profession but a traveling bag.

The dining room door burst open and the two little boys tumbled into the room, with Minnie following them, her dark skin wearing an ashen tinge.

"Is Daddy goin' fishin'?" demanded Bill. "He said next time he went fishin' we could go, too."

Susie caught her breath and for a moment turned from them. Steve bent over the boys, rumpling their hair, grinning down at them.

"Next time Daddy goes fishing you're going, too. Daddy's going away on business. You two kids take care of Mommie, you hear?" he ordered, managing by some miracle to keep his voice deceptively gay in their ears.

"Oh, sure, we'll take care of Mommie," said Junior importantly.

"I take care o' all o' dem, Mist' Steve," said Minnie

harshly. "You ain't never done nothin' wrong—better no-body try to tell me you is."

"Thanks, Minnie." Steve's voice was husky and he dared not try to speak to Susie. He only held her close and hard against him for a moment, and then he thrust his way past the two men and out into the cold gray morning.

PART TWO

14. Making Her Way

In A DRAB, DREARY ROOMING-house near the railroad station in Savannah, a woman with lank dark hair, a face that was innocent of make-up, wearing a nondescript dark dress and looking a million miles removed from the sleekly beautiful, smartly groomed Laura Weston, flung the newspaper away from her and stood up, walking to the grimy window. She looked unseeingly out at a painfully depressing view of scabrous brick walls and overflowing garbage cans.

Her mouth was a thin ugly line and her eyes were narrowed until they were little more than slits. She stood for a moment, smoking, dragging the smoke down deep into her lungs, and then letting it dribble out as though quite unconscious of what she was doing. She stubbed out the cigarette at last with a vicious twist and walked to the old-fashioned bureau and leaned close to the peeling mirror above it.

Carefully, as though she had never seen the face that looked back at her, she leaned close and, her fingers lifting the dark, lank hair studied it for betraying signs of the gleaming golden radiance so successfully hidden beneath it.

She stepped back at last, satisfied that the job of dyeing she had done last night had been successful. Her mouth twisted wryly at the thought of the hair-coloring fad that made it so easy for a woman, in just a few hours and unaided, to change the color of her hair so completely. But she hated the effect—this drab plain woman who looked back at her.

Merely by leaving off her expensive girdle that had controlled her voluptuous figure so enticingly, she seemed to have gained pounds; she winced at the little roll of fat around her hips, but knew it for an excellent disguise. In the cheap, worn dark suit, the rayon stockings that were an insult to her really beautiful legs that had hitherto been clad in the filmiest of nylons, the low-heeled cheap shoes, no one in the world would ever recognize her. She felt quite sure of that. She had changed all her appearance except her height, and by stooping slightly, her body was given a weary look that seemed to reduce even that. Tinted glasses concealed the blue-gray of her eyes. Oh, she had done a good job of losing Laura Weston—and just in time, too!

That damned "Ann Smith!" Only her name was really Claire Lafferty, according to the papers. She was a woman of great wealth; thinking of that, Laura remembered the two thousand dollars the other had given her and ground her teeth in rage. What a set-up she would have had for blackmail if only the woman had lived and carried out her plan to adopt her own baby!

But there was no sense in following that line of thought. The woman was dead; the "nursing home" was closed; and Steve Prescott was being held in jail as a material witness and there was an ominous hint that the charge against him might be very serious indeed. There was every likelihood that even if he escaped a long prison sentence, the medical society would take action against him, suspending his license, perhaps—or even withdrawing it permanently. That would serve him right, Laura told herself viciously. Him and his damned scruples that had precipitated the debacle of all she and Dr. Harmon had so carefully and painstakingly built up! And that little pudding-faced Susie —Laura's hand went up almost absently and touched her jaw, so vivid was the memory of the blow Steve had delivered when she had previously called Susie a "pudding-face."

Well, he was paying for that now, and he would go on paying for it. Because they would never find Anna. Of that she was sure. And they would never find *her!* She patted the little roll of fat over her flat stomach and hips. No one would ever guess that it was a money belt containing twenty thousand dollars in bills of large denomination! But the thought of the money brought her anger; it could so easily, given another year like the last two, have been a good deal more. Destroying her records had been a bitter blow; but she had not dared keep them. She must rely on her memory for the machinery to carry on the blackmail that was so much a part of her business. The fools who wanted babies so badly that, denied the regular channels of the accredited agencies and impatient of the long delays, the red tape, they were willing to pay handsomely for babies whose mothers had been willing, even anxious to pay to have disposed of—of such fools had her "business" been built. And the people who had adopted the babies and come to love them as their own—they were always good for a threat, delicately veiled of course, that the rightful mothers had suddenly wanted to reclaim the babies, and so were willing to pay again and again in order to keep the children.

Yes, it had been a most lucrative "business." Her job in Steve's office had given her some excellent contacts; she had known, from her work at the hospital, how to reach carefully selected unmarried mothers—Anna had been wonderful in that field. She swore savagely at the realization that it was all gone now, and that she must start over again. She looked about the drab, ugly room; for a moment she saw her luxurious apartment, her beautiful clothes, all put away now in storage and she'd never dare claim them. The damned police! But at least they had no idea where she was. And the time had come for her to make her next carefully planned, shrewdly executed move; ahead lay another "business" to be built up and carefully tended.

She picked up the battered suitcase she had bought at a pawnshop when she stepped off the train, threw into it with loathing the two or three cheap dresses she had bought next door to the pawnshop, and added the ten-cent-store toilet articles. Her mouth was thin with bitterness as, once more, she visualized the apartment—the racks of expensive clothes, the delicate feminine fripperies—and swore at her own weakness for remembering such things. In the life that lay ahead, the new "business" that she would build up would provide more beautiful clothes, another luxurious apartment, all the extravagant frivolities that she loved. She had only to keep her head, to move carefully and cautiously, always taking one step and considering the next three before she budged.

The frowzy landlady, exactly the sort one would expect to find in a place like this, was apathetically stirring the top layer of dust on the ragged hall carpet when Laura went down the stairs, carrying the battered suitcase. The landlady eyed her sharply, avid curiosity in her near-sighted pale eyes.

"You're not leavin' us?" she asked plaintively.

"I've got a job out at the paper mill," said Laura curtly. "Have to find a room closer to the job."

"Well, I hope you ain't expectin' a refund—'cause I don't give refunds," whined the landlady defensively. "I could 'a' rented your room if I'd 'a' knowed you was moving before your week was up."

For a moment Laura wanted to tell her viciously that she was welcome to the three dollars to which she was entitled. But that would not be in character with the type of person she, Laura Weston, must pretend to be. To a woman who dressed and looked as Laura did three dollars would be a sum worth haggling over.

"I think that's pretty mean of you," she said hotly. "After all, I'll have to work a week before I'll get paid—and—well—I need the money."

The light of battle glowed in the landlady's eyes, and Laura met her halfway and when it was over, Laura was walking down the street, swinging her suitcase, her mouth grim, but with a dollar and a half refund in her shabby cheap leather bag, while the landlady stood on the dirty door-steps and hurled insults after her . . . .

From then on, Laura moved carefully, covering each step that lay behind her before she took the next one. Though occasionally she grew impatient and felt that she was wasting valuable time, and that she was perfectly safe and could move freely now, she forced herself to go on being cautious. Until at last on a bright, warm day near the end of the winter season, she reached the Florida "Gold Coast" city which had been her objective from the first. But not even Anna—most of all, not Anna—had ever heard her so much as mention the name of the town.

Somehow along the way she had abandoned the battered suitcase and the lank black hair. She was now a dashing red-head, smartly dressed in impeccable taste. Nothing flashy or "glamorous." She looked every inch the well-bred lady to whom anything ostentatious in dress would be thoroughly distasteful.

She began by finding a convenient comfortable apartment. Next, she opened an account at the nearest bank with half her remaining money. She was still too cautious to put all of it in the bank, for her past experience had taught her the necessity of having an ample supply of cash on hand should the need for flight arise. Of course, without Anna to hamper her, she felt moderately certain that given a fair run of luck to which certainly she was now entitled, flight was not likely to be necessary. She looked about her and settled down to her campaign.

There was an attractive cocktail bar not too far from her apartment. She had already discovered that it attracted well-dressed, well-heeled men and women and she had formed the habit of dropping in shortly before the dinner hour for a glass of sherry. This she would sip appreciatively and in silence and then would depart.

Until one evening while she was finishing her single glass of sherry a man whom she had been watching discreetly came over to her, and smiled tentatively down at her.

"I'm Phil Colter," he introduced himself, smiling. "I run the place here."

He was a big man, perhaps forty, brown as mahogany, very fit-looking and his white dinner jacket with the dark red carnation in the lapel set off his good looks to perfection.

Laura let her eyes slide over him, coolly, appraisingly; her head lifted haughtily, but there was a sparkle in her eyes that made Phil's blood flow just a little faster.

"Now, really, Mr. Colter. Do I look like a pickup?" she drawled disdainfully.

"If you did, baby, you'd never have got past the door," Phil told her and there was a touch of grimness in his voice. "There aren't many places around town like this one. And I aim to keep it that way."

"Unescorted women on the make are not allowed?" there was a touch of amusement in her voice.

"Definitely not. There are plenty of other places for them to work. I keep the Tokay as the sort of place where women alone, down here for 'the cure,' may feel free and relax."

"The cure?"

"A ninety-day residence that provides relief from the bonds of matrimony that have begun to—chafe," said Phil dryly.

Laura laughed lightly.

"I'm not here for a divorce, Mr. Colter. Just a holiday," she assured him dryly.

"Swell! I was hoping I could see a bit of you while you are here—but usually there is the complication of a jealous husband in the background who for one reason or another does not care greatly for his wife taking 'the cure.' "

"With me, it's a complication you can forget," she assured him. But there was a thoughtful look in her eyes as they swept over him measuringly. "My complication—is something very different, I do assure you."

"I'm a great guy for handling complications other than jealous husbands," he told her and his eyes on her were warm and admiring. "And what about that drink?"

Laura twirled her tiny glass thoughtfully for a moment and then she laughed softly.

"It seems to be—well, an occasion. Why not?" she agreed lightly.

Phil signaled to the barman in his crisp white coat and bent lower above Laura's head saying softly, intimately, "And perhaps dinner?"

Laura studied him appraisingly and let a small, provocative smile touch her lovely mouth.

"Why not?" she said again with a small shrug as she accepted the sherry the barman offered. She lifted it in a gay toast to Phil.

15. A Delicate Condition

AFTER THAT FIRST DINNER, AND A superlative affair at a private club where Phil was received with such devoted attention that Laura felt quite sure he either owned the place or had a sizable stake in it, they saw a good deal of each other. Laura had decided to be careful that he should not see her often enough to become tired of her. He was proceeding cautiously, too, and it amused her to realize that he still could not quite place her in the social scale, that he could not quite make up his mind just what and who she was. She had given him her name as Lorna Shaw; she had not pretended it was really her name; she had simply, that first evening, dropped the name between them and let him use his own judgment.

He was quite helpful in as many ways as she would allow him to be. When he discovered that she did not have a car and offered her the use of his own, she had demurred and explained that she had been intending to pick up one of the well-kept, very good used cars that are always so plentiful at the close of the season. Phil had promptly taken her to a friend of his who kept a fleet of smart, expensive cars for hire during the season, and had helped her select one at a price that made her widen her eyes a little.

Phil laughed.

"Oh, he's not cutting prices just because you are a friend of mine, nor am I slipping him a few bucks under the table to make up the difference between the actual price of the car and the one he's asking you," he answered the unspoken thought in her mind. "He gets such fantastic prices for renting these cars to the winter residents, who want a car to drive around while they are here for the season, but don't want the bother of driving one down, or back home when the season is over. By the time the season is ended, Dave has already got back what the car cost

101

him, from rentals. And what you are paying him for the car is pure velvet."

Laura had laughed and written the check for the car and had driven it out of the lot and parked it in front of her apartment.

Phil had followed in his own car and when she had parked her new-used one, he came and stood beside her.

"This calls for a party, don't you think?" he suggested.

"My buying a car?" she teased.

"Well, why not? You're going to have a lot of fun with it—" He leaned closer and put his hand over hers where it lay on the steering wheel. "Look here, Lorna—or whatever your real name is—aren't you getting just a little tired of this—'hands off'—business? I'm crazy about you and you know it. You tell me no one has any strings on you—and me, I'm free as air. So why the hell don't we have some fun?"

"I've been having fun. You've given me a wonderful time—" she told him softly, realizing that the moment towards which she had been building was approaching. "I'm very grateful, really."

"Hell, you don't have to be grateful to any man who shows you a good time, Lorna. The favor is all on your side," he told her and she saw his dark eyes redden with flames with which she was so familiar that she all but laughed in his face. "Look, you've never seen my place. How about having dinner there tonight? My chef's quite a guy. The way he can dream up wonderful food isn't even funny. Later, we can do whatever you like."

Laura's eyes held his for a long moment and there was promise in them and suddenly she smiled.

"Whatever I like?" she repeated softly.

Phil stepped back and his jaw hardened.

"That's what I said—and it's what I mean. You call the turn—that's the way I play it," he told her almost harshly.

"Sounds like fun, Phil. Thanks. About seven-thirty?" she suggested lightly and saw the eager delight that leaped into his dark eyes.

He gave her the address and went back to his own car. And she sat for a little, smiling, her eyes narrowed, her busy mind clicking with the exciting thought of "this is it!"

She had never dressed more carefully. Trying several of the new frocks she had bought, her choice fell at last on a filmy black chiffon and lace over a flesh-pink slip so delicate that it was hard to decide where the slip left off and Laura began. The gown was cut very low; any woman with superbly moulded breasts like hers, she had told herself when she bought the dress, was a fool not to make the most of plunging necklines. Now, adjusting the dress, she managed to lower it still more and her smile as she studied herself in the mirror boded no good whatever to Phil Colter's self-control.

The night was almost uncomfortably warm and as she trailed a black chiffon stole about her shoulders and went out to her waiting car, she thought of what Atlanta must be like on this March evening. Cold and blustery, a stinging wind—and for just a moment she wondered if Steve was in prison. But the thought was one she dismissed almost the moment she was conscious of it, for that part of her life was done with and whatever happened to him and that simple sap of a wife of his was no more than he deserved!

She found the house whose number Phil had given her, and for a moment she sat at the wheel of her car, staring at it, puzzled. Because it was a small house, not more than six rooms, though two of them were upstairs rooms. It occupied a lot entirely enclosed with a tall hedge in front, and a stucco wall, splashed with the inevitable bougainvillaea at the back. Tall feathery bamboos were visible at the back, and the gate through the wall at the side indicated a patio. Somehow, she had pictured Phil living in some sort of swank bachelor apartment—yet this, she supposed, was more discreet and Phil was obviously a man who valued discretion.

As she turned the key in the door of the car, standing on the sidewalk, the door of the house opened and Phil came down the flagstone walk that neatly bisected the unnaturally green lawn, with its borders of blossoming shrubbery.

"You're ten minutes late," he accused her happily. "I've been standing at the window with my nose glued to the pane."

He cupped a hand beneath her elbow and marched her up the walk to the house. "This, my friend, is not exactly the sort of place I expected to find you occupying."

"What did you expect?"

"Oh—something lush and—er—exotic in the way of a bachelor apartment, probably on the Via Parigi—" she laughed.

"I bought this a couple of years ago. No switchboard operator, no elevator. Just quiet and privacy," he told her cheerfully, his hand warm on her arm as he guided her down two steps into the long living room that opened, through french doors, into the patio she had been quite confident would be here.

She looked about her, taking in the expensive furnishings that were in superb taste but indicated money lavishly spent, and she nodded.

"I like it," she told him quite sincerely. "It's very nice."

Dinner was, of course, served in the patio. A small but expensively perfect patio, complete even to the small fountain at the far end, splashing with a silvery tinkle into a bowl where fat goldfish swam decoratively. There were borders of bright-hued begonias around the fountain base, and there were white, purple and pink asters glowing among phlox and petunias, scenting the air with delicate fragance.

The middle-aged Negro man, in his spotless white coat, who had cooked the food and now served it, was all that Phil had boasted. Most of the time he was expressionless, well-trained; only now and then Laura caught a faintly speculative look in his dark muddy eyes as he glanced at her.

When dinner was over and they were back in the living room, with a handsome Georgian silver coffee-service on a low table in front of Laura, she had filled the egg-shell thin cups for both of them. Phil lit cigarettes and leaned back, as though filling his eyes with the sight of her. And Laura was thoroughly aware, of course, of the very enticing, provocative picture she made against the dull gold brocade of the cushions behind her.

"You really are an amazing person, Lorna," said Phil, ending a small silence that had been born of some vague, indefinable tension growing between them.

"Am I?" her smile was teasing, provocative, her eyes narrowed.

Suddenly he put down his cup and came over to her. She waited for him, still with that small, teasing smile curling her lovely mouth. He took her cup, put it down and lifted her to her feet and into his arms with a hungry passion that would no longer be denied. His mouth burned on hers, until her heart, that cool, well-trained, severely disciplined organ, stirred slightly.

She let him have his way with her until he had drawn her down on the couch and his caresses became bold, demanding, intimate. He was so sure of her surrender! Suddenly she twisted herself free of him in a lithe, unexpected movement and was away from him, leaving him sprawled ignominiously on the couch, staring at her in ludicrous dismay that slowly deepened to a savage anger.

"What the hell is this all about?" he demanded savagely. "You're no innocent, untouched virgin. You're no coy young thing building a fire to warm her hands and then running innocently away before she gets singed. You knew why I wanted you to come here tonight—if you didn't intend to come through, then why the hell—"

"I'm in a delicate condition," she tossed the cool words into the midst of his fury as though they had been of no particular importance.

She saw that the words rocked him. For a moment he went on staring at her, his eyes dark with fury, his face set and white with thwarted passion.

"You're what?" he asked at last as though quite sure he could not possibly have heard her correctly.

She nodded. "You heard me—I'm in a family way," she repeated. "That's why I have to be—well, careful!"

He could not doubt the calm, cool conviction in her tone. He turned sharply away from her, his shoulders rigid beneath the well-tailored white dinner-jacket.

She waited, cool, alert, her expression under careful control. Almost she held her breath; this was the moment towards which she had been working since that first night in the Tokay when he had spoken to her. If she had guessed wrong—her hands, hidden in the filmy folds of her black, smoky chiffon gown clenched tightly, but she kept her face calm and without expression.

He spoke at last, without facing her, tossing the words over his shoulder, his voice taut and ugly.

"How the hell did a smart gal like you get herself caught?"

"I was playing a long shot," she said quietly. "I thought I could get him to marry me—but I was a fool to think he'd hold still for such a play."

Phil turned, his balled fists jammed deep into his pockets, and his grim, set face, ashen behind its traditional mahogany-bronze—a man like Phil Colter would as soon be caught in public without his pants as without that carefully nurtured "Florida tan"—and his eyes raked her from head to foot with a cold, measuring glance that made her smile faintly.

"Oh, it doesn't show—yet," she drawled coolly. "It's not quite three months, although I told him it was more."

Phil was still savage with frustrated lust.

"How'd it happen?" he demanded curtly.

Laura's eyebrows went up and she allowed herself a faint smile of satirical amusement.

"Well, really!" she mocked.

"I mean—how did you make such a mistake in your estimate of him? Crazy in love with him, of course—"

She laughed outright at that in such frank amusement that some of the dark anger melted from his face.

"Love? Phooey! Don't be childish," she sneered. "He was—and is—quite a big shot. Tons of money—and he's old enough to know his way around. He was pretty crazy about me, but I came from the wrong side of the tracks, and he was convinced that he had not been my first lover; so it never occurred to him that I might want to marry him. I figured that he was about the age where a man should begin to yearn for—oh, a home where he could entertain his friends, a good-looking wife who knew the score, and the patter of little feet. So I—I let it happen."

"And?" demanded Phil.

She lifted her shoulders in a shrug and let her hands fall.

"He suddenly had business elsewhere—damn him!" she said through her teeth. She had planned the story so carefully, rehearsed every tiny detail until, caught up in the necessity of convincing him, she almost managed to convince herself.

Phil turned and walked the length of the long room and back again, his head sunk, his fists still jammed in his pockets.

"And what happens now?" he demanded.

"I haven't had much luck in ridding myself of the little stranger," she told him through her teeth. "I—came down here away from everyone I knew, because I couldn't face the horse-laugh I'd have gotten from my friends and acquaintances. I thought maybe I might find a doctor who would—well, listen to reason and a good stiff fee. But— they're a bit hard to find, when you're a stranger."

Phil eyed her sharply, his brows drawn together.

"You don't want the kid?" he demanded sharply.

She stared at him in shocked reproof.

"Now, I ask you—is that a sensible question? Can't you just see me, all wrapped up in formulas and diapers and—ugh!" she shuddered in honest disgust at the idea. (And risked a deep and ardent breath of relief that the whole thing was a fabrication of lies!)

Once more Phil paced the room and back, and then he halted to lean on the back of a tall chair, and to eye her sharply, his brows still drawn together in a dark frown.

"So you would like to be relieved of this—impediment to your career," he drawled slowly, and there was a contemptuous sting in his voice.

"You're putting it rather crudely," she told him icily. "Naturally I'd rather avoid the complications of motherhood. But after all, it's my problem, not yours. I merely wanted you to understand that I am not—a tease! I find you exciting and very disturbing and I feel you could be—a hell of a lot of fun. But under the circumstances, you can see that too close a friendship is hardly—well, not the indicated thing!

"And now, if you'll excuse me, I'll say good night," she tossed over her shoulder as she moved towards the door, catching up the long filmy black chiffon stole that was flung across a chair.

"Wait a minute," protested Phil, and she paused and turned to him, her brows raised in a delicate inquiry she did not bother to put into words.

Phil came closer and his eyes clung to her bared shoulders with an avid look that made her feel that he was caressing them with his hands.

"Look, if I help you out of this by putting you in touch with a fellow you can trust absolutely—how generous would you be in return?" he demanded with brutal frankness.

Laura smiled faintly.

"What do you think?" she murmured softly.

Phil breathed deeply, and his hands jammed tighter in his pockets. As his eyes slid over her, they were filled with a naked, brutal hunger that made Laura feel again that momentary brush of panic. This man would not be an easy lover; she would have her hands full with him. But not even that thought made her hesitate a moment in going ahead with the plan she had so carefully made.

She met his stare, smiling, her eyes warm and limpid and filled with a provocative promise that tensed the man's nerves to a screaming need for that exquisite voluptuous body. But he could wait, and it would be worth waiting for. He nodded at last and turned away.

"I'll make the arrangements and let you know when and where," he said over his shoulder.

Laura felt a momentary weakness from the tension of suspense; she feared that after all maybe she had made a costly mistake. Any mistake would be more than she could afford now, after she had put so much spade work into carrying her plan to its completion.

"You are going to help me?" she stammered and her voice sounded shaken, incredulous.

Phil turned and stared at her.

"Sure—I'm going to help you—and then you're going to be mine—for as long as I want you; is that clear?"

16. Woman's Doctor

TWO DAYS LATER SHE PARKED HER car in front of a modest bungalow on the mainland, across the lake from the winter-resort city. She looked about her and wrinkled her nose uneasily. It wasn't at all the sort of place she had expected. In a shabby, run-down section of the city, within a block of the railroad, cluttered and untidy. For a moment she knew a touch of hesitancy, but then she locked her car, got out and went up the walk to the door of the bungalow that swung open to her as she mounted the rickety steps.

The man who greeted her was spectacularly good-looking, but his face was touched now with fury.

"What the hell are you trying to do, bring the police down on me?" he snarled as he closed the door behind her and stood glaring. "Sitting out there in your car looking scared to death and not quite sure whether to come in or run away—"

"Are you Dr. Burton?" she asked icily.

"I'm Nick Burton, yes." His jaw hardened as he denied the title. "Come on in. You're Lorna Shaw—or so you say."

He marched ahead of her down the narrow hall that bisected the small, shabby, down-at-heel house. He held open the door of an examining room that was moderately clean and aseptic looking.

He turned and looked at her.

"Get your clothes off," he ordered and stalked away.

When the door had closed behind him Laura stood quite still for a moment, her head cocked in amusement. He was so fantastically good-looking, tall and sun-bronzed. He had a thick shock of straw-colored hair with a slight but perceptible wave—she could imagine him carefully cultivating that apparently careless wave. His eyes were

110

startlingly blue in his brown face and she was quite sure that once he stopped frowning, and grinned at a girl, he could make her heart flutter.

She wondered at a man like this going in for illegal medicine. Even if he were a very bad doctor, any man with his looks should have had no difficulty in building up a tremendously prosperous business among impressionable women alone.

Suddenly she laughed under her breath, and, with her eyes impish, began to disrobe. When he came back a little later, knocking first at the door before he came in, she lay on the examining table, in the proper position, clad only in the coarse sheeting robe that she had found in a corner.

Her body thrilled to Nick's expert, impersonal touch. From her own training as a nurse, she realized his manner was perfect; that of a man trained to dedicate himself to medicine so that a woman's body in its most intimate revelations was something to be examined and handled as though it were some inanimate thing of stone or wood.

She lay watching him, the impish look in her eyes and her body thrilling to a startling degree each time he touched her. So she was prepared for the moment when he straightened, his handsome face dark with angry amazement, looking down at her exquisite body as though he found nothing about it to excite his interest.

"What the hell's the pitch?" he demanded savagely.

Her eyebrows went up and her smile was soft and sweet.

"Why, Doctor—I don't know what you mean," she purred sweetly.

"You're no more pregnant than I am," he accused sharply.

She laughed.

"Of course not," she agreed, watching him with that impish amusement he found so puzzling.

For a moment he stood staring down at her and then he flung the robe over her and turned sharply to the door.

"Get your clothes on," he ordered. "I'll be waiting in the reception room for an explanation—and it had better be a damned good one."

"It will be," she flung after him as she rose from the examining table and began to dress.

In the waiting room, small and shabby with its cheap unpainted wicker furniture and the faded cretonne, he was standing, smoking, his face a black cloud of anger and suspicion.

"What's this all about? Colter didn't send you—" he burst out when she came into the room.

She dropped into a chair, crossed her lovely legs that were bare and already delicately tanned, and lit a cigarette. She looked up at him, smiling through the fragrant blue smoke.

"Oh, yes, he did, Doctor," she said gently. "But then, you see, he thought I was pregnant."

His eyes were hard and cold as blue marbles and there was a stiffness to his jaw line that indicated a burning anger as well as frightened uneasiness at his position.

"But why the hell should you tell Colter such a lie— what did you hope to gain?" he puzzled, and his very bewilderment increased his savage fury.

"Because I had to find you," she purred sweetly.

Instantly he was still, like a hunted animal that scents a trap and brings up all his skill in dodging pursuit to help him.

"Oh? And why did you have to find me?" he asked at last.

"Oh, not you in particular, Doctor," she hastened to relieve him. "Just—a man who could be persuaded to, shall we say have a tolerant viewpoint towards women who don't wish to start raising a family."

"Look," snapped Nick and his hand shook slightly as he lit a cigarette and smoked it in short, angry puffs. "Let's cut out the double-talk, and the cute stuff—and get down to cases. What the hell is this all about?"

Laura said quietly, "By all means, Doctor—let's. It boils down to this—I think you and I could work together very smoothly; I think we'd be quite a team. So I'm offering you a proposition."

Some of his uneasiness but none of his bewilderment was gone.

"Such as what, for instance?" he demanded shortly, his eyes seeming to bore into her.

"This business of yours is a mug's game, Doctor—you know that as well as I do," she told him almost serenely. "What does it get you but a few measly bucks, and always with the hot breath of the law on your neck. There's ten times, a hundred times, as much money in—the other end of the business. A maternity home for unmarried mothers, with a guarantee of placing the little offspring in good homes with—well-heeled people who, for one reason or another, can't adopt a baby through the regular welfare agencies—"

Nick was staring at her in such complete amazement that Laura stopped, shrugged, and waited for his mind to catch up with her. It took him a matter of moments, and at last he said, nodding, "So that's your racket. Black market in babies."

"It beats what you're doing."

Slowly, unwillingly he nodded.

"Sure—I won't give you any argument there," he admitted. "Still, the kind of set-up you're talking about calls for capital—a lot of it. Protection money for that kind of racket comes high."

"Then why pay protection?" argued Laura reasonably. "Why not just play it smart—and safe?"

"Which would be about the neatest trick of this, or any other century—except I can't see where it's possible—"

She smiled at him.

"Oh, I don't know—I did very well for a couple of years and didn't pay a dime to anybody," she told him quietly.

His eyes flew wide at that and travelled over her slowly, taking in the supple, deliciously moulded body beneath the filmy blue and white silk frock, the proud upward thrust of the beautiful breasts, the flatness of stomach that melted into neatly rounded hips and flowing thighs and the brown bare legs.

"You ran one of these places?" he asked at last.

Her mouth twisted with bitterness of memories she hated to face.

"I did," she told him curtly.

"Oh?" his eyebrows went up and he waited expectantly.

She shrugged.

"I was scuttled," she told him grimly. "By a doctor who couldn't stay off dope—and another who was afflicted with scruples."

"That happens," he agreed cautiously.

There was a small silence between them, and they eyed each other appraisingly.

"Well?" demanded Laura at last, her voice taut.

"Well, what?"

"Oh, don't give me that—do you or don't you want to go in business with me?" she snapped at him harshly.

He was thoughtful, wary.

"With Colter handling the protection?" he asked cautiously.

"With Colter knowing not a damned thing about it."

Startled, he protested, "Hi now—you're Colter's woman—"

Outraged, she was on her feet, her eyes blazing.

"That's a damned lie! I'm nobody's woman—" she cried harshly.

Cold-eyed, he looked her over.

"Colter sent you to me," he pointed out.

"Because I told him I was pregnant—"

He nodded slowly.

"And he wanted to be damned sure you didn't hang the rap on him," he said grimly. "Smart cookie, Colter."

"Colter wants me," she admitted almost reluctantly. "He knows that he can't have me until—" she shrugged, letting the sentence fall without ending it.

"You're a pretty smart cookie, too," he agreed wryly. "If you're planning a double-cross on Colter, let me warn you now he'll never take it. He's quite a guy. Packs a lot of weight in this territory."

"Are you afraid of him?" she sneered contemptuously.

"Hell, yes, I'm afraid of him," he admitted without shame. "You would be, too, if you knew what was good for you."

Puzzled, she studied him curiously.

"Are you trying to tell me that Colter is head of the rackets down here?" she demanded.

"Hell, no! He's a very reputable citizen with a lot of standing and stuff—one of the heavy tax-payers, and all that," said Nick grimly. "Has a piece of just about every club and recreation center—I use the word loosely—in the three adjoining counties. Works with the cops, not against them; and his word goes with them. If he says 'lay off' they lay off; if he says 'give him the works'—the next stop is usually jail."

Laura was thoughtful.

"He told me about you," she said after a moment and was delighted when she saw Nick start as though she had thrust a long and very sharp pin into him.

"Told you what?" he snapped harshly, his eyes wary, definitely uneasy.

"Oh, about the trouble you had up north—when you were within a few months of completing your Senior Interneship in Obstetrics. How you botched a piece of 'homework' and the girl died. A student nurse, wasn't she?" drawled Laura sweetly.

She saw Nick's face go gray behind his sun-bronze.

"Damn him!" he said through his teeth. "Damn his lousy soul to hell and back."

"Oh, don't be so upset—I'd be the last one in the world to squeal on you," she drawled insolently. "I was looking for someone like you, and—well, I think you and I could do each other a lot of good. I know you are competent, or Colter wouldn't have sent me to you. He wants me well and fit, free of any complications. And the best is what I'm looking for."

"I'm deeply touched by your confidence in me," sneered Nick, still badly rattled by her knowledge of his past.

"Well, I guess that's that," she told him coolly. "If the proposition does not interest you, I shall simply have to tell Colter that you were not cooperative, and get him to locate someone else for me."

"Meaning that you'll see Colter throws me to the wolves!" said Nick savagely.

She turned towards the door and hesitated. Then suddenly she turned swiftly and came back to him, soft and warm and very tempting, all sweetness and coaxing.

"Look, Nicky, why should we battle like this?" she pleaded, the change in her so sudden and unexpected that it startled Nick. "I need you in this job. I've got some capital—I know all about it. I've got a list in my head of several couples who will pay handsomely for a healthy, normal baby to adopt. Finding unmarried mothers who want to place their babies for adoption isn't difficult. Colter will probably send you one occasionally and it will be your job to talk her out of getting rid of the baby, and into allowing it to be placed for adoption. You can convince her it would be safer for her. We might even slip her a few bucks if it seems advisable—believe me, Nicky, I know all the angles."

"But you got caught once," Nick pointed out.

Her face hardened and her eyes went cold.

"A damned fool doctor got caught—you'll notice he is the one who is serving time in prison, while I'm free as air," she reminded him.

"I had the thought in mind. That it was the medico who was left holding the bag, not you."

She laughed tensely.

"That was because he had ethics and scruples—also a wife and a couple of kids," she said. "He had everything to gain by squealing on me; you have everything to gain by playing ball with me, and nothing to lose—because you and I know that sooner or later you are going to run afoul of the law with this cheap, shoddy business you're in. Why live in a dump like this, existing on the fees you pick up, when I'm offering you wealth and luxury with less risk than you're taking for peanuts now?"

She saw that he was listening with more interest and suddenly, very winning and gay, she said lightly, "I've been riding around town, getting the lay-out. I have a couple of spots in mind that look ideal for our kind of set-up. Why not ride out with me and have a look at them and then think things over? Though why you need to think things over when I'm offering you such a deal, I'm sure I don't know."

Nick looked down at her, uneasy.

"D'you know, I have an idea you're dynamite," he said at last.

She laughed, knowing she had won.

"Well, you aren't exactly what I'd recommend as a cure for a nervous breakdown, pal," she teased.

17. Black Market

THE HOUSE SHE FINALLY CHOSE was, both agreed, ideal in every respect for the sort of business she planned. High on a ridge overlooking the city spread below, it was a leftover from a previous real estate boom. A Spanish stucco, four rooms downstairs, two rooms, each with bath, upstairs. Enclosed by a high stucco wall painted a dark green that wind and weather and several hurricanes had lashed into a pale, faded remnant of color. The patio, enclosed by the wall, was a tangle of weeds and overgrown shrubbery. But the house inside was in good condition.

Laura was able to arrange a year's lease, at a good price with the privilege of making whatever repairs and alterations she considered necessary. If the realtor who arranged the lease wondered why a smartly dressed, well-bred woman who seemed to have plenty of money was willing to pay well for so unattractive a house, he was too sensible of his luck in arranging the deal to ask questions.

It was Phil Colter who asked the questions. But Laura had braced herself for them. She had her story well in order when she dined with him at his house a week or ten days after the night she had told him she was with child and he had sent her to Nick.

"What's all this I hear about you leasing a house on the mainland, Lorna?" he asked after dinner, when they were alone in the living-room and she had just poured his coffee.

She looked up at him, surprised.

"How did you know?" she asked innocently.

"Oh—things get around," he answered and she saw the suspicion in his eyes.

She laughed and made a little deprecating gesture, as

she picked up her fragile coffee cup and leaned back in her cushioned chair.

"I meant it for a surprise," she said gaily.

"It was a surprise, all right. You and Burton seem to be getting on famously together."

Laura lowered her white eyelids above eyes that were suddenly sharp and wary, and carefully lightened her voice.

"Oh, well, he's rather nice. And of course I'm grateful because he took care of me so beautifully," she said casually.

"He did take care of you, then?" said Colter. "I'm glad. I had expected you to—well, to let me know how things were."

"Oh, yes, he did a beautiful job," said Laura and added quietly, "He's quite competent. Too bad he got into trouble—"

"So I understand," said Colter. "At least I've heard no complaints from any of the customers I've sent him."

"His is rather an unpleasant business," she said at last.

"Oh, I don't know—it's a very necessary sort of job, it seems to me. Kids who lose their heads and get into trouble —somebody ought to lend 'em a helping hand," said Colter, his voice almost expressionless.

Laura looked up at him at last.

"I imagine you find his job very necessary—" she said at last, deliberately.

"If you mean that I make use of his services to keep me from being a father—that's a damned fool thing to say. I happen to be a little too smart to allow that kind of a rap to be hung on me. The girls I send him—they are usually girls who work for me at the clubs and restaurants, the—various enterprises in which I have an interest. Also, some of my boys get in jams with their girl friends—I'm afraid they keep Burton fairly busy. I haven't heard him complaining of being hard up."

Laura kept silent for a moment, thinking hard and then she looked up at him again, her mouth thin.

"Have you ever thought, Phil, that maybe it might be smarter for the girls to go ahead and have their babies— and place them for adoption—" she began slowly.

Colter said sharply, "Cut that out! What the hell are you bucking for—a federal rap? Because that black market baby racket is strictly poison and I'll have no part of it. Sure, I know there are people who will pay big money to adopt a kid, but it's against the law—the federal law, baby. Once the kid is taken across the state line, the F.B.I. moves in. And no one who has any part in any of my businesses is going to lay himself—or herself—open to such a rap as that!"

Laura said icily, "Please don't shout."

Deflated, Colter studied her. His eyes still desired her, but the desire was overlaid now with a wary, suspicious caution that frightened her, because she could ill afford the suspicion, the hostility, of a man as powerful as Phil Colter.

"Sorry," she told him with a humility that brought an acrid taste of bitterness into her own mouth. "I didn't mean to be nasty. I just wondered—that's all."

Colter's jaw was set and hard as he carefully put down his coffee cup and studied her sharply.

"I didn't mean to shout at you," he apologized ungraciously. "It's just that it makes me so damned mad when some fool suggests some play that brings down the F.B.I."

Laura's laugh was light and not as convincing as she tried to make it.

"Thanks for the advice," she said lightly. She stood up and her head was high. "And now I think I'd better be running along," she told him smoothly. "After all, a little more of this kind of conversation and we'd be quarreling. And that's something I don't want to happen."

She walked towards the door, Colter watching her until she had almost reached it before he said peremptorily, "Wait a minute, Lorna."

She paused and turned, her eyebrows raised in polite inquiry.

Colter came to her and stood looking down at her and now the anger and suspicion were gone from his eyes and replaced by that look of naked, almost painful desire she had seen there before.

"Look here, Lorna, I'm not ordinarily a patient guy," he told her. "But I've been putting chains on myself until you were—well, ready to listen to what I have to say."

For a moment she did not raise her eyes and in the folds of her thin skirts her hands clenched tightly. She had known that this moment was inevitable; she had braced herself for it and had felt that it was not going to be too bad. Not too high a price for the need she might have for him later. But now that it was here—her mouth was dry and her nerves crawled with distaste. She was not a passionate woman, for all the warm lushness of her looks. Passion was something fools played around with, always to their loss. A two-edged sword that never failed to leave its painful mark. She had surrendered her carefully cherished body only when she had had no other means of getting what she wanted, as with Steve that night that now seemed a century ago. And now—

She drew a long deep breath that lifted her breasts enticingly beneath the filmy folds of chiffon that veiled them and looked up at Colter, throwing into her eyes all the semblance of ardor that she could command.

"Yes, Phil?" she murmured huskily.

"I'm crazy about you, Lorna. Damn it, you know that. You've been turning me on the spit very expertly until I'm done to a turn—and now it's pay-off time, Lorna. I can't wait any longer," he told her and his voice was rough with passion. He drew her swiftly into his arms and held her crushed hard against him, his mouth ravaging hers, burning his kisses on her white throat.

Somehow she managed to fight down the shudder of revulsion that shook her, for she dared not defy him now. But into her mind crept a thought she had not dreamed possible—if only it were Nick Burton who held her so— Nick Burton who demanded the surrender of her cherished body! The realization that if it had been Nick, she would have given herself with a joyous abandon of which she had never before thought herself capable, shook her so badly that even in the tight pressure of his arms, even through the red haze of passion that gripped him, Colter was aware of the involuntary shiver that went through her.

But he believed it her rising response to his desire, and was elated.

"I'm going to hang you with diamonds, baby," said Colter, babbling on and on. "Anything your little heart desires. I might even—why, hell, I might even marry you. If you like."

Almost roughly she pulled herself from his arms and got out of bed, standing slim and exquisite in the dim-lit room as she reached for her things.

"Thanks, but I don't like," she told him dryly. "That marriage stuff is strictly for the birds. I want no part of it—ever!"

Her back was to him so she did not see the swift expression of relief that touched his face and was gone. To be replaced by an oddly curious, speculative glance that for a moment wiped out the ardor in his eyes.

She refused to let him drive her home, and Colter did not insist. She went down the stairs and out into the early dawn, still very dark but touched by the whisper of breaking dawn.

She did not drive straight to her apartment. Instead she turned the car along Royal Palm Way and parked facing the ocean, scowling into the darkness, her teeth sunk hard in her lower lip. Because she was still unpleasantly shaken by the realization that, like any silly sap of a high school kid she had fallen in love; and with Nick Burton of all men!

It was one of her few really black hours. Heretofore, when things had gone wrong, she had always been able to figure a way out. But even in her mental turmoil and confusion, she knew that there was only one way out of this mess; that was flight! And she quailed at the thought of running away from Nick!

There should have been uneasiness about Colter's reaction to her tentative suggestion about the maternity home with its side line of babies for adoption. But there was no room in her thoughts now save for this ridiculous and somehow frightening complication of her sudden yearning for Nick. It didn't help to remind herself savagely that it was a purely physical thing, that there was no love to

it, in the sentimental understanding of that word. It was
—lust. Sheer animal lust. But just the same, it had steel
claws that tore at her until she was weak with the need
for Nick's body possessing her own.

She was jerked sharply to a consciousness of where she
was, when suddenly a shadow loomed up beside the door
of her car and a flashlight played over her. She gave a
small cry of shock and fright, and the man switched off
the flashlight and in the grayness of the breaking dawn
she saw the familiar blue, brass-buttoned uniform of a
policeman.

"Trouble with your car, miss?" he asked her politely.

"No, certainly not!" Her voice was sharp, edged with
annoyance. "Is it against the law to park here for a little
and watch the sunrise?"

"Of course not, miss," said the policeman amiably.
"It's not too safe, though, for a lady alone—couple of
hours before sunrise. We patrol the area pretty regularly
but at that there are some tough characters around that
might pop up, when we're at the other end of the route."

She had herself under control now, and she drew a
deep breath and forced herself to say courteously, "I'm
sorry. You're very kind. I guess I'm pretty foolish. I'll go
home and let the sun rise by itself."

"That might be wiser, miss," said the policeman and
stepped back politely as she switched on the ignition and
started her car. But as she backed and drove away, she
glanced at the rear-vision mirror above her driving wheel
and saw him still watching her car as she wheeled it into
Royal Palm Way.

18. One Lover Too Many

SHE SHOWED NICK OVER THE HOUSE a few days later. She had already brought her luggage over and was living in the house. She watched Nick anxiously, trying not to let him realize her anxiety, as she took him on a tour of the rooms.

When they were in the patio, neat and tidy now, freshly groomed and with potted plants about, lending color until the newly transplanted begonias and marigolds began growing, she watched him, waiting.

"Quite a set-up you've got here," he said at last. "What does Colter think of it?"

"He hasn't seen it yet," she said curtly. "I wanted you to be the first."

"That's very sweet of you," he said dryly. "I'm deeply touched. Funny, though, that Colter let you spend this much money."

"Colter's not paying my bills," she flashed at him hotly. "I am paying them myself. Nobody has any strings on me! Nobody—do you hear?"

"Sure, I hear. Maybe you're right, but—you're being a bit of a fool to splurge so heavily on a gamble like this," he told her and now there was a grimness in his tone that struck at her sharply. "Because it is one hell of a gamble."

"I'll get it all back—and plenty more, once we start business."

"Let's forget that 'we' business, lady," Nick interrupted swiftly. "I want no part of anything as risky as this thing you've cooked up."

Laura sneered at him, anger blazing in her eyes.

"What you're doing, of course, is as safe as death and taxes, I suppose," she flashed at him.

124

"So long as nobody squeals—and the kind of gals who come to me aren't likely to squeal. They like their own pretty little necks too much," he pointed out. "And with Colter on my side—" He lifted his drink and swallowed appreciatively, so completely at ease that she all but hated him for a savage moment.

"You seem to be scared plenty of Colter," she sneered.

"Sure I'm scared of him. He's all that stands between me and a long prison stretch." He shuddered at the thought and drank again.

Suddenly he put down his glass and turned to face her. His eyes were grim and cold as though she were some bit of furniture, instead of a lush and very desirable woman who was his for the taking.

"Look, Lorna—or whatever your real name may be," he began. "There are a hell of a lot of complications about this plan of yours. Oh, sure, I know you realize that—but there's one thing which may have slipped your mind. The little matter of time."

Taken by surprise, she stared at him.

"Time?" she repeated and saw his handsome mouth touched by a fleeting grin that was not amused, only cynical.

"Sure," his tone was light. "It takes nine months to have a baby. I never touch a girl who comes to me after the third month; that leaves at least six to go before delivery of the infant and your being able to cash in on the adoption business. What are you going to do with these girls during that six or seven months stretch?"

"Is that what's worrying you?" she laughed at him in bitter derision. "The girl goes on with her job, whatever it is, coming to you—here, of course—for the usual pre-natal care and treatment. She enters the 'nursing home' shortly before the baby is due. What could be more simple than that?"

"But Colter's girls are supposed to show up for work within a week or so after the alleged operation. How are they going to keep him from knowing there hasn't been any operation? I am, of course, taking it for granted, knowing Colter as I do, that he will have no part of this cute little set-up you've got rigged here."

"He will not!" agreed Laura stiffly. "Why should we split the take three ways when you and I will be doing all the work?"

"Now I know I want no part of it," stated Nick flatly, and stood up. "Thanks for thinking of me, and all that— and it's been nice knowing you—but this is where I get off."

She stared dumbly as he walked with long purposeful strides across the small patio and into the living room. And suddenly she was on her feet following him, calling his name so that he turned halfway across the long, tastefully furnished living room and looked back at her.

"Nick," she said and her voice was husky with the burning desire she could no longer keep out of it and her eyes brimmed hotly with it. "Nick—don't go. Please don't go."

Nick frowned, turning and studying her.

"I'm crazy about you. Nick. Oh, don't look so dumbfounded!" her voice broke and she struggled to regain it. "Oh, I know I'm a fool— and you've had scads of other women and—I'm just one more woman to you. But—Nick, you're the only man I've ever really wanted. Nick, stay here with me—please stay with me!"

Nick's eyes narrowed, and swept over her in the thin silken slacks that she wore, moulded to her lovely body in a revealing fashion that could scarcely have been duplicated even by a wet bathing suit. He saw the rapid, uneven rise and fall of her lovely bosom and for a breathless, shaken moment she detected naked, hungry desire in his eyes. The next moment he had drawn a deep breath and backed away a step from her, putting up one hand as though to evade any gesture she might make to touch him.

"Oh, no, baby—you don't take me in like that," he told her harshly. "You're wasting time, trying to use your body—and what a body!—to get me involved in your schemes. Papa's too smart to fall for that, baby . . . only . . . damn you, you know I want you like hell—"

She swayed towards him, fumbling with the thin silken shirt until she had slipped it from her shoulders and was offering herself, her face white with desire, her eyes blazing

"Oh, Nick—don't be a fool! Don't deny us what we both want so terribly. Nick, Nick—please, Nick—"

Never in her wildest dreams had she imagined herself not only offering her body, but demanding its appeasement from any man. Yet when Nick caught her close and held her so tightly that she could scarcely breathe, she knew a rapture beyond anything she had ever known or dreamed could come to her. Nick was a perfect lover, and through the exquisite turmoil of her enchanted senses, she was too caught up in intoxicating delight to realize that his perfection as a lover indicated a vast deal of experience.

That wasn't important. Nothing was important beyond one fact. She, who had previously trafficked only cold-bloodedly and with inner disgust in such episodes as this, for the first time in her life was fulfilled and transported by the shared passion so perfectly completed.

Afterwards, when the transports were over, and they lay side by side, close-held, basking in the delicious languor of fulfillment, he looked down at her head that lay against his naked shoulder and there was something almost of awe in his voice.

"If it wasn't such a damned fool thing to say, I'd almost feel like saying—you behave like a girl with her first lover."

She laughed in delicious enjoyment of the moment.

"It isn't such a damned fool thing to say, darling, because in all that really matters, you are my first lover," she told him and when he made a small, derisive sound of amused disbelief, she turned her face to his and pressed her cheek hard against him.

"Oh, I'm not trying to pretend I'm snow white," she admitted quite honestly. "But you are the first man to whom I ever gave myself in love."

Somehow, he was touched by that, a humility so completely at variance with all that he had known of her.

And there was something very like compunction, if one could imagine a man like Nick Burton experiencing such an unlikely emotion, in his kiss. . . .

Long after he had dressed and gone, she lay alone in the big double bed, her hands laced together beneath her head, her eyes unseeingly on the open windows, where the tops of trees moved faintly against the hot blue sky.

She wasn't kidding herself. Nick would have no part of this business she had planned for both of them; but —he was Nick and she was mad about him, and he had enjoyed their passionate interlude. She knew men well enough to be certain that she had given him a satisfaction that despite his many affairs, must have been rare indeed. And because of that, she had a hold on him. She wasn't kidding herself; he would come back to her. Because he would need her as she would need him—again and again. And—she stretched luxuriously like a drowsy, cream-fed cat curled up beside a warm hearth—he would, sooner or later, see her scheme the way she saw it; and they would be in business together. The thought brought a delicious warmth and peace and she slept soundly as she had not slept in many nights.

She was awakened by the sound of the telephone and sat up groggily, surprised to find that she had been sleeping though it was only now dusk. She heard the phone again and pulled herself out of bed, wrapped a robe about her and drowsily lifted the receiver.

"Well, hello there," said Colter's voice and there was an element of relief in it. "I was about to give up and decide you were not home."

"I was taking a nap," she admitted.

"Alone, I hope," said Colter. "I've missed you."

"It's nice to know I've been missed," she put all the coquetry she could dredge up above her dislike for him into her voice. "I've been terribly busy getting my house in order."

"I can imagine," said Colter, and added significantly, "I was hoping to be invited over to see it—soon."

There was nothing to be gained by fencing with him. She had to keep in his good graces for she had no idea when she might need him. And only by playing a very wary game could she keep him unsuspicious and sufficiently interested in her to be sure he would heed her call.

"Well, it isn't quite straight yet, but why don't you come over for cocktails? I'm a foul cook, or I'd invite you to dinner."

"No man could ask for a fairer invitation than that," said Colter, obviously pleased. "And about dinner—there's a new club opening on the highway tonight. Why don't we have dinner there?"

"Sounds wonderful," said Laura with all the enthusiasm she could muster. "I'll get myself all done up in my most fetching garb!"

Said Colter happily, "I can hardly wait."

He was right on time and as she opened the door to him, his eyes swept her in an appreciative glance that took her in from the top of her shining red-gold head to the tips of the silver slippers that peeped from beneath billowing skirts of dark green tulle and chiffon, sprinkled with silver embroidery.

"Hi, you're too beautiful to be real," he told her and swept her into his arms, with a stark hunger that repelled her.

"If we're going to the opening in style—please, mister, don't handle the merchandise," she laughed and led the way, her skirts swaying about her slender body like a giant inverted bell, into the living-room.

"We'll open the club in style," he told her fondly, and accepted the cocktail she poured for him. His eyes clung to her body with an avid hunger that made her all but recoil.

"And now you must see my house," she told him proudly. "I can't show you the bedrooms—"

"Why not? Most interesting part of a house," he assured her, his voice throbbing with desire as he bent his head and kissed her shining hair where the curls sprang up from her white neck.

"Because they're not finished yet. All in a mess. I don't want you to see them until they are perfect," she assured him gaily, and led him on a tour of the ·lower floor, which he inspected with gratifying approval and admiration.

"I've always wanted a kitchen like this," she told him. "Though I'm sure I don't know why, since I can't even boil water without scorching it around the edges."

He came close to her and his hands went out for her, and his face tightened slightly as she evaded him laughingly.

"No one as beautiful and decorative as you are should ever be expected to be at home in a kitchen!" he told her huskily.

At last, with a hidden sigh of almost abject relief, she managed to get him out of the house and into the car. The thought of his caresses, while her body still throbbed with the remembered ecstasy of its complete and prodigal surrender to Nick's urgent demands, was more than she could endure. And as they drove off she was calculating coldly, carefully, how to avoid yielding to him even after he brought her home from the club-opening. She was going to need him, she knew; but she would hold him off— risky though she knew that to be. She had to hold him off, now that she had discovered the delight of giving herself joyously to some one like Nick, whose passion aroused a blazing response so completely at variance with the smothered disgust she had always just barely managed to conceal in the arms of other men.

19. Haze of Jealousy

THE CLUB WAS LUSH AND EXPENSIVE and just about what she had expected. A place where the cover charge was high enough to keep out those who could not afford to lose handsomely, and without squawking, in the well-equipped gambling room that was a matter-of-course part of it.

Colter was greeted with great warmth by the plump, middle-aged, balding maitre d'hôtel, and ushered to the best table in the big room, which had a terrace overlooking the ocean. The dance floor was of good size though it was already crowded when Laura and Colter reached their table. Champagne appeared as if by magic and Laura arched her eyebrows laughingly at Colter.

"Nothing but the best for you tonight, my love," he assured her expansively and his eyes, hot and demanding, crept over her so that she felt as though they were fingers, probing, caressing, seeking. She set her teeth hard behind the smile she managed to force, as Colter went into consultation with the waiter about their dinner.

She had lit a cigarette and was glancing idly, incuriously, over the dancers when suddenly her eyes were caught and held by a sight she was ill-prepared at the moment to face—Nick Burton, spectacularly good-looking, his beautifully tailored white dinner jacket setting off to perfection his bronzed, handsome face! The girl in his arms was a lovely, fragile bit of Dresden china: shining pale golden hair, powder-blue eyes the exact shade of her clinging satin frock, that was so low in front, Laura told herself viciously, that she could have nursed a baby without disarranging it in the least. The girl looked sleek, expensive, well-kept; there was about her an air that Laura knew meant money—lots of it—and no doubt social position as well. Laura was too shrewd a judge to mistake the woman, for an instant, for anything but what she was—one of the wealthy winter colonists, lingering on after the height of the mid-winter season had passed.

Colter finished giving the order to the waiter and turned to Laura. She was studying Nick and the lovely blonde with such sharp, angry concentration that Colter frowned, as though startled, and an odd look came into his eyes, even as he followed the direction of her gaze, and recognized Nick.

For a moment that Laura was too absorbed to properly assay, Colter watched her, and when at last she became aware of his look, she felt the color rise high in her face and she had to clench her hands tightly beneath the table to control their trembling and for a moment she could not steady her voice sufficiently to dare to try to speak.

"Nick seems to be steppin' out high tonight," said Colter dryly. "He's quite a lad."

"Who is the girl?" asked Laura and in her own ears her voice sounded harsh and stiff.

"Marcia Courtney," said Colter almost curtly. "Lovely, isn't she?"

"That tramp?" the words were bitten between Laura's white teeth, so filled with bitterness that Colter's eyes narrowed a little as they clung to her white, angry face.

"No woman who is worth as many millions—in her own right, be it added—as Marcia Courtney, could ever be called a tramp," he corrected her dryly.

"She's been married and divorced half a dozen times —she's notorious—" Laura knew she was being a fool and knew that her savage, betraying jealousy was thick in her voice but for the moment she had completely lost her head.

"Sure. But if Nick can make the grade with her—more power to him, don't you think?" said Colter coolly, his eyes hard and cold.

Laura gave a short, ugly laugh.

"You surely don't think she'd marry him?" she spat viciously.

"Why not?" drawled Colter and now every vestige of warmth was gone from his voice and his face was set. "Nick's quite a lad with the ladies. And he has expensive tastes that Marcia would no doubt be happy to cater to."

"An illegal doctor!" said Laura through her teeth, her voice little more than a thread of sound, stifled by jealous fury.

"That's not a pretty term," drawled Colter. "I admit there are some women who have cause to be very grateful to Nick for relieving them of undesirable complications. You, I think, were one of them."

Through the red haze of fury and jealousy that fogged her mind, something pierced like a white hot light. She realized that Colter's manner had chilled; that his eyes upon her were wary and hostile. She knew, with a frightened sinking of her heart, that she had made a terrific mistake in letting him guess that she was emotionally interested in Nick.

She forced a laugh, picked up her glass and drank thirstily, and shrugged.

"Oh, well—of course I'm grateful to Nick. It's just that I was so surprised to see him stepping out in such a rarified atmosphere," she said lightly, and could not keep back the spiteful words, "After all, perhaps Marcia is one of his customers. Who knows?"

"Who, indeed?" agreed Colter and said politely, "Would you care to dance?"

"I'd love it," she said in strained relief at getting away from the table, where he could look with such disconcerting sharpness into her eyes. But when he took her into his arms at the edge of the dance floor, he held her almost casually, almost as though she had been a middle-aged and unattractive spinster with whom he was performing a duty-dance he'd be glad to have ended as soon as possible.

Her eyes followed Nick and Marcia, who were obviously having a marvelous time. But she tried to move closer into Colter's arms, and to stir her body slightly to make him aware of her. He seemed to pay no attention whatever to such maneuvers, and at last she made herself look up at him and smile gaily.

"What is this—dancing by remote control?"

"This is a respectable joint," he tried to match her gaiety. "I prefer not to be flung out of it for—illegal passes in public."

"Discreet, aren't you?" she tried to sound gay and mocking, but her eyes followed Nick in spite of her efforts to meet Colter's steady regard.

"An essential of public conduct, don't you think?" he suggested. And as the dance ended, he bowed formally to her and turned, his hand barely touching her elbow to guide her back to their table.

As they reached the table, Nick and Marcia, passing, stopped to say hello. Marcia greeted Colter as though well acquainted with him and looked with friendly curiosity at Laura as Colter presented her.

Nick stood a pace behind Marcia, who was making gay meaningless conversation with Colter, and for a moment Laura's eyes met Nick's with the impact of a blow. Her face was white and twisted, and Nick, as though startled, raised his eyebrows a trifle and a smile touched his mouth for an instant and was gone almost before she could be quite sure it had ever been there.

The red fog of jealous fury was back again, and she cursed Nick Burton mentally, with every vile epithet to which she could lay tongue. A few hours before, they had been together in her bed and he had evidenced the keenest possible delight in possessing her as no other man had ever possessed her; her body was raging with the need for his; yet here he stood, casually at ease, obviously very contented, on top of the world. She wanted to murder him in some slow and very painful manner that would take a long time; but more than anything else in the world, she wanted to be possessed by him again.

Marcia ended some brief, amusing story she had been telling Colter, to which he had listened with amusement and interest. She turned to Nick, slipping her hand through his arm with a proprietary gesture that, to Laura, was like a blow beneath the heart.

"Come along, darling," she said happily. "I'm way past due to lose a lot of money in this gambling hell."

Colter pretended to wince and said in a tone of pain, "Please, Mrs. Courtney—I beg of you!"

But Marcia only laughed, nodded pleasantly to Laura. She and Nick moved away in the direction of the doors that opened, if one was known to be "perfectly safe," into the gaming rooms.

Colter glanced at Laura and the waiter came, serving the first course of their dinner. By the time he had finished his devoted ministrations and departed, Laura had managed to get some small grip on herself, but she was trembling slightly, so that her fork clattered a little as she lifted it.

"Nervous?" asked Colter politely.

"Nervous? How silly—of course not—I've a bit of a headache—" she hated herself for the old, threadbare excuse and saw by Colter's expression that it rang as falsely in his ears as in her own.

"Too bad. May I get you an aspirin?" he suggested, and she caught the hint of boredom in his voice. A tiny warning bell rang far back in her mind. "Careful, Laura, you damned fool!"

She took up the glass of champagne, smiled tautly above it, and said gaily, "Thanks, I find this much more— helpful than aspirin."

The reply was so feeble Colter paid it the attention it deserved, which was the merest lift of the brows. She exerted herself to be gay and amusing, and to pretend she was having a hell of a lot of fun. But when the meal was over, she had eaten almost nothing and her gaiety was becoming almost shrill and hysterical.

"Since you have a headache," said Colter when he had settled the bill, "I'd better take you home."

"I'm afraid I've been very dull company—" she apologized, trying not to let him see how welcome his suggestion was.

"Oh, I wouldn't say that," drawled Colter pleasantly, but his eyes were cold. "It's been a most instructive evening."

She looked up at him, startled, but he was holding her chair. He led her out of the place and into his car. She chattered as they drove back to her house, and he answered politely, almost in monosyllables. When the car stopped in front of her house, she braced herself and turned on all her charm. He helped her out of the car and walked with her up to the door of the house. He took her key, unlocked the door, handed the key to her and stood back.

"But—aren't you coming in?" she protested, startled and disappointed. She had braced herself to yield to him and to use every atom of her feminine charm to win him out of his black mood.

"Thanks, not tonight. You're much too tired," he told her formally.

"But—I'm not—a bit. Do come in, if only for a nightcap—" she heard herself pleading.

"Thanks, not tonight. I'll take a rain check on that, if I may," he said.

And while she stood, open-mouthed, watching him, he walked down the flagged path and through the patio gate into the street. She went on standing there, cold and frightened, until the red tail light of his car had twinkled out of sight around the corner. And then slowly, thoughtfully, she turned and went into the house.

She dropped into a deep chair in the living room and, free of Colter's wary, hostile eyes, gave way to the bitter fury and pain torturing her since that unbelieving moment when she had seen Nick dancing with the very wealthy and social divorcee, Marcia Courtney.

There was no room in her mind for any thought of the danger in alienating Colter, as she knew she had done. She could win Colter over—later. Now there was only the bitter jealousy of knowing that Nick had gone straight from her bed to Marcia. That she had, for the first time in her shrewd, careful life, given herself in joy to a man who had dismissed the gift as of no more importance than the body of a two-dollar street walker.

There was shame, humiliation in her jealousy; she was desperately hurt in her pride. That arrogant pride that had made her sneer at women who were less chary of their passion; she had never, until with Nick, given herself without the knowledge that she would gain a great deal from the despised gift. But with Nick it had been— well, indescribable. She had not dreamed that such rapture was possible, and to know it had meant nothing to him drove her to frenzy.

At last, near dawn, exhausted and spent, she broke another long-established rule and swallowed two sleeping tablets. She fell into bed, welcoming the blessed oblivion of drugged sleep that would ease for a little while the aching demands of her body, the tortured torment of her jumbled thoughts.

20. Payment in Kind

IT WAS LATE AFTERNOON WHEN SHE awoke, feeling logy and dull-minded and with a throbbing headache. For a while she lay still, until her mind fought its way back to clarity. And then when all was clear to her again, she got out of bed, her mouth thin and twisted, and reached for her robe. She caught sight of herself in the mirror and was unpleasantly startled at what she saw.

Her white, haggard face, the dark circles beneath her eyes, made her, for one of the few times in her well-cared-for life, look her real age. An ugly presentiment of what the future—and the not too far distant future, at that—would bring. Another thing, her hair needed re-touching, because at the roots the pale gold was faintly discernible. She shivered and turned away from the mirror. In the bathroom she turned on the shower and stood under it, shrinking but grim-lipped, until her body was rosy with the tingling cold. She toweled herself vigorously, and looked down at the carefully nourished beauty in which yesterday Nick had seemed to delight—yet while her surrender was still only hours old, he had gone straight to that Marcia!

She dressed very carefully in a crisply tailored shark-skin slack suit, made up her face with the greatest possible care and brushed her hair into shining order. This after taking a hand-mirror and standing in the dying sunlight beside the window to carefully touch up with a tint-stick the roots of her red-gold hair.

She hadn't admitted even to herself what she was going to do. But when she went downstairs, she carried a large flat envelope bag under her arm and her car keys were in her hand.

As though the car knew its way without being guided,

she drove straight to Nick's house, working her way through the afternoon traffic with almost automatic skill. Her conscious mind was wholly absorbed in the coming scene with Nick. She would plead; she would abase herself; she would crawl in the very dust if she had to; but she had to know the delight of Nick's love-making. She could not live without it; and she was sickened and terrified of the force of desire. She had had an arrogant assurance of her lure; she had never failed with a man when it had suited her purpose to gain from him something she wanted by the surrender of her body. And it was unthinkable that now, when she wanted Nick so much, she could be denied.

She got out of the car in front of Nick's house and went up the walk, unconscious of the grimy, dingy neighborhood. Not even seeing the man, clad in a cotton undershirt and ancient cotton trousers, who sat on the steps of the house next door, and who watched her with a lively appreciation of the proud thrust of her curves against the thin stuff of her slack-suit.

She rang the bell and waited, her whole body tense. There was no answer and she rang again. Still no answer, and now she put her finger on the bell-push and kept it there, leaning against it, hearing the clamour of the bell deep inside the house. But there was no other sound.

Suddenly, her self-control vanished and she beat with her clenched fists on the door, forgetting everything but the desperate need of coming face to face with Nick.

The man who sat on the steps next door had been watching her curiously, and now he got up and came to the edge of the narrow drive that was all that separated the two houses.

"No use banging away like that, lady," he told her, and she caught her breath and whirled about, startled, to face him. "He's not home."

"I don't believe you!" panted Laura, lost to everything but the urgency of seeing Nick.

The man's curiosity deepened but now there was a chill in his eyes.

"Well, look, sister, it's nothing to me whether you believe me or not. But I'm telling you the guy left couple of hours ago—in a swell-looking car with a good-looking doll!" he told her shortly.

She seemed to sway and her face was so white and desperate that the man, about to turn away, hesitated, frowning. Uncontrollably, Laura whirled about and once more pounded savagely on the closed door.

"Look, sister," snapped the man and took a step towards her almost threateningly. "I'm telling you the guy ain't home. Now, beat it, or I'll call the cops. Get me?"

Her breath came in a small, sobbing gasp, and at last she turned and stumbled down the drive to her waiting car. But even as she stood beside it, struggling for enough self-control to get into it and drive away, a car she had every reason to know very well indeed, for it was Colter's car, drove slowly past, and for a moment Colter looked at her from behind the wheel. A long, level-eyed glance that chilled her blood; and then, without a word, he drove quickly away and Laura stood watching as the car slid out of sight.

For a long, long moment she stood there, the bitter, acrid taste of shock and fear in her mouth. And then she became aware of the man behind her, who was standing at the steps watching her. She stumbled into her car and set it in motion, driving automaton-like, dazed and sick and shaking.

How she got back home she could never afterwards remember. But eventually she found herself back in her living room, huddled in a shaking heap of shock and bewilderment. How *could* she have made such a fool of herself? Last night, when she had betrayed to Colter's cold, watching eyes her jealousy and anger with Nick; that had been, of course, the worst kind of a dead give-away. And then today—how long had he been following her? How much of that absurd, ugly scene on the steps of Nick's house had he witnessed? Had he seen her beating with her clenched fists on the door of Nick's house? Had he seen her driven away by the sloppy-looking, curious-eyed man next door? Remembering the look in Colter's eyes as he had held his car still before driving away, she shivered and put her face in her hands. What an utter fool she had become! After all her years of shrewd, careful planning, of cold analytical forging ahead towards her goal of "big money," stepping on and over anybody luckless enough to get in her way! She had got herself into this spot simply because of an unruly passion for a man to whom she had been just another woman—one of many before her, and no doubt a great many after her!

She needed Colter desperately! Fitting up this place, remodeling, equipping it, had taken far more money than she had planned. The original bankroll with which she had arrived here had shrunk outrageously; there had been the car, the expensive apartment where she had lived, the expensive clothes. The palms of her hands were wet with sweat and she rubbed them down her thighs, scarcely conscious of what she did.

At last, out of the depths of her shock and anger and humiliation, was borne a desperate hope that Colter might want her badly enough for her to be able to retrieve with him some of the lost ground. It was a hope that sent her up the stairs to her room where she sought carefully among her formal and provocative gowns. She dressed with painstaking care, making herself her most alluring. Delicately she perfumed herself in the manner she had long ago learned, with hidden contempt, was most calculated to make men desire her. And when she had finished, she nodded in grudging approval at the alluring image of herself looking back at her from the mirror, then went swiftly out to her car.

It was almost seven and the traffic had thinned, except along the highway to Miami. She crossed the high arched cream-colored bridge, whose amber lights were already aglow, and turned into Cocoanut Row, away from Royal Palm Way. She parked the car in front of Colter's house, and saw with sharp relief that his car was in the driveway, which meant that he was at home.

She braced herself as she went up the flagged path between glowing beds of rose and white and red begonias, and lifted the handsome brass knocker.

The door opened after a moment or two to reveal the

dignified houseman who looked at her with eyes in which no recognition showed; beyond him, across the hall, soft light glowed in the living room and there was the tinkle of ice in thin glasses and a woman's laugh. Laura tensed at the sound.

"Yes, miss?" said the houseman, his voice colorless, polite.

"Mr. Colter, please—"

"Who's calling, miss?" asked the man.

"Damn you!" Laura barely managed to smother the words, and to steady her voice to say "Miss Shaw."

"One moment, miss—I'll see if Mr. Colter is in," said the houseman, and to her unbelieving fury closed the door neatly in her face, leaving her standing on the steps!

The woman's laugh still echoed in her ears. For all that it had been a light, gay, soft laugh, it meant that Colter was not alone. The terror creeping along her veins made her shiver despite the warmth of the night.

The man opened the door again and looked at her without expression.

"I'm sorry, miss, but Mr. Colter is not at home," he said.

For a moment that could only have been seconds but that seemed to Laura to stretch endlessly, she stood quite still. Then she heard Colter's voice, warm and teasing and ardent, and again the woman's soft laugh.

"Damn you—I hear him!" she said harshly, thickly.

The houseman's expression did not change. He merely eased the door shut in her face, and she heard the bolt slip home.

She stood there unbelieving for a long, long moment. Colter had refused to see her; yet he had another woman with him. If she needed anything to convince her—which, by now of course she didn't—that he was completely and for all time through with her, this was it.

Conscious at last of the agonizingly humiliating position she was in, she turned and went back down the flagged walk to her car. She slammed it in gear and whirled about to Royal Palm Way. She drove to the sea front and parked, staring out at the turquoise-blue haze of the restless water.

Her jealousy of Nick had been augmented now by her fury at Colter's treatment of her. And underneath that, there was the uneasiness of realizing what a spot she had got herself into. She had worked coldly, carefully, deliberately to get into Colter's good graces. Then when she had had him right in the palm of her hand she had been the world's most complete fool, had thrown everything away for a golden hour or two with a man who cared so little for her he had not given her a second thought.

Out of her growing fear and deepening bitterness, came a thought she would ordinarily never have tolerated for an instant. There was just one way that she could get even with both Colter and Nick. She could go to the District Attorney with what she knew about Nick, and she could also point out that Nick had worked under Colter's protection. She did not believe that Colter's "protection" would cover Nick's activities.

The thought frightened her and she tried to put it from her. But long after she had driven home and paced the floor until she was exhausted, the thought kept bobbing up. It would be a measure of exquisite satisfaction to put Nick Burton behind bars; it would appease some of her bitterness against Colter for his treatment of her tonight if she could see him squirming in hot water. And she knew that her story could accomplish both. She was too obsessed by the necessity to avenge herself on them for their behavior towards her, to stop to realize the grave danger to herself in such a betrayal. She took sleeping pills again, knowing she must have some rest, even if it was only drug-induced. And fell asleep with the comforting thought that tomorrow she would set in motion action which would pay both Nick and Colter for the humiliation they had visited on her.

21. Final Fling

It WAS NOON BEFORE SHE FOUGHT her way out of that drugged sleep. She made coffee and forced herself to drink it. She studied her plan of bringing down punishment on Nick and Colter, and was too over-wrought to see anything but the simple justice of it. They had used her shamefully—they had insulted and humili-ated her—and now she must see them punished or never know another moment's peace.

At first she planned to go to the District Attorney's office. But when she was dressed and ready to leave the house, she knew that was more than she dared risk. There would be questions; she might slip up; reveal more than she wanted to reveal. More than she dared reveal.

An anonymous letter? She was too impatient to wait for a letter to be delivered. She wanted action; wanted something done to Nick and to Colter *now*. She got into her car and drove into town. Parked in the big City Parking Lot in the park facing the lake, and walked along Clematis Street to a big drugstore where there was a row of telephone booths. She believed it was difficult, per-haps impossible, for the police to trace a phone call that came from one of these booths.

She found the number in the book fastened by a chain to the ledge outside the booths. She entered a booth and closed the door tightly. Even after she dropped a coin and dialed the number she was tempted to put down the receiver, give up the idea—but before she could follow that impulse, a voice spoke in her ear, brisk, pleasantly impersonal and she heard herself saying huskily, "I have some information for the District Attorney."

"Who's calling, please?" the voice was not quite so im-personal now.

144

"I—my name would mean nothing to him. I don't dare give it—but—it is information he would like very much to have." She steadied her voice by a terrific effort, yet there was in it a note of urgency that made the receptionist say quickly, "One moment please."

And then a man's voice said quickly, "Yes? You have some information for me?"

"I—yes," she drew a long, hard breath. "I wanted to tell you there is a man named—Nick Burton," she gave the address.

"Yes?"

"He is—well, an illegal doctor," said Laura huskily.

"You have proof of this charge?"

"You'll find all the proof you want at his place," she told him, and now her bitterness against Nick had hardened and strengthened her voice. "Also, you'll find that he is protected by a man named Philip Colter, who operates the Tokay Club."

And even as the man's questions came at her, she put down the receiver and opened the door of the booth. Her knees were trembling so that she could scarcely stand but she braced herself with the feeling that she must get away from this place as fast as possible.

She managed to reach her car in the big parking lot; she fumbled open the door and all but collapsed inside it. She propped her elbows on the wheel and put her face behind her shaking hands. She was furiously, fiercely, glad that she had betrayed Nick and Colter. But now that she had taken the irrevocable step of revealing them, stark terror bathed her in an icy flood. Her mouth was dry at the realization of what she had done, and she had no illusions about Colter's reaction once he knew about it. Nick she wasn't afraid of; there was nothing Nick could do. She would enjoy visiting him in prison and laughing her head off at him. But Colter—he had power and could be a dangerous enemy. Yet powerful though he might be in this resort city, she did not believe he had the power to beat such a rap as this. He might wriggle free eventually —but he would be very busy for a while. And while he was busy, she must see to it that she got far, far away from here. Covering her tracks as carefully, as successfully as she had done when she had slid out on Steven Prescott.

The thought of flight, the necessity of making every move count, sent the terror into the back of her mind and she steeled herself for what had to be done. Back to the house; she would pack and remove all her expensive personal effects. She dared not use the car; it would leave a trail too easy to follow. She could not dispose of the surgical equipment that had cost so much more than she had been actually able to afford; she would have to flee with far less money than she had had when she left Atlanta. Yet—she needed all the money she could get.

Uneasily she considered that for a moment, and then with a sudden recklessness, she remembered a used car lot on the way to her house with a big weather-beaten sign, "We Buy and Sell Used Cars." If she moved fast she might salvage that much!

The used car dealer eyed her curiously when she stepped from her car and asked curtly, "How much?"

"Bad time of the year to sell a car," he objected.

"I have to sell it," she told him harshly. "I've just had a wire calling me North—an emergency. There's no time to drive. I'm taking the next plane and I need ready cash."

The man nodded and made her an offer so ridiculous that for a moment she almost swore at him in savage fury. But he knew that she would accept it and when she demanded cash instead of a check, he shrugged and walked back to the small, ramshackle building that served as an office.

She accepted the money, thrust it into her bag, and the man offered, "Drive you home, lady? One of the boys will be glad to."

"Thanks—no. The bus runs right past my door," she told him curtly and walked swiftly away.

The man watched her curiously. But her papers had been in order; proof of ownership, registration—and when he had gone back to the office, he had telephoned the dealer from whom she had bought it, being assured that the car was not "hot" and that if she wanted to sell it, she had the legal right. Funny, though a lot of funny things came into the life of a used car dealer in this town.

Laura walked several blocks before she dared hail a taxi in order to go to her house. She thrust a bill at the man and went hurriedly up the walk. Her hand shook as she tried to fit the key into the lock but at last she managed to get the door open. She ran swiftly up the stairs, and to her own room, where she hauled down her smart new luggage and began packing swiftly. Reaction had set in, of course, from the cold fury that had driven her to report Nick and to implicate Colter. She had burned her bridges—she had cut off her nose to spite her face—if she had kept her mouth shut, she could have stayed on here, built up a business, reaped a harvest from the money she had invested. But in order to appease a purely feminine rage, she had thrown all that away.

The fact that it was too late to do anything about it only added to her misery, and her hands shook badly as she packed swiftly, her mouth a thin, bitter line.

When she had finished, and her bags were downstairs at the foot of the steps, she walked through the house. The bright brand-new electric refrigerator and range in the kitchen, the good-looking furniture she had chosen so carefully—it was bitterness to have to leave it all behind. The ease with which she had disposed of the car, for all that it had brought her so little, tempted her to a move that she would not have made had she been less overwrought.

She dialed a number on the telephone and when a voice answered, she asked swiftly, "Do you buy good used furniture?"

"Sure," answered the voice.

"I have to leave for the North immediately—an emergency," she explained swiftly. "I've just furnished this house and I may not be back. Would you care to come out and give me an estimate on the furnishings?"

"What time tomorrow?"

"Not tomorrow—it must be now, immediately," her voice was harsh. "I'm taking the next plane."

"Well, I dunno, lady."

"Then I'll call somebody else—"

"It's almost four o'clock—"

"And I'm almost ready to leave."

"O.K., lady. What's the address? I'll send somebody out with a truck."

"And the cash."

"Well, I'll see—"

She put down the receiver and lit a cigarette. She sat down because she was shaking so that her knees threatened not to support her. She was not taking too much of a risk, she told herself, in waiting to salvage what she could from the sale of the furnishings. She was going to need every penny. She would have to go a long way off— perhaps California—somewhere where there would be no danger of her past catching up with her. And again she berated herself savagely for losing her head and making that telephone call. Tardily she realized that while she had avenged herself on Nick and Colter, she herself would suffer as much as they would. Oh, they'd probably go to prison; she was viciously sure that Nick would, though Colter might be powerful enough to wriggle off the hook. But she would be a fugitive, fleeing—fearful—

She had behaved like an utter damned fool! Worse, she had behaved like an ordinary woman! She had lost her head—that smoothly clicking, coldly efficient brain which had served her so well up to now.

She paced the floor, unable to sit still. And after what seemed to her many hours of waiting, she heard the sound of a car in the drive, and ran to the door, thinking it the furniture man.

She swung open the door, and stood rigid.

The car in the drive was a neat dark coupe of a popular make. The man who faced her in the doorway was middle-aged, neatly dressed, inconspicuous looking, but his eyes were cool and wary. "Miss Laura Weston?" he said politely.

And such was her agitation, her shocked state, that she answered automatically, "Yes?"

The man's eyes smiled briefly, and he brought his hand out of his coat pocket, and opened it to give her a flash

of a badge that startled her so that she clung to the door
to keep from falling.

"I'm Henderson, of the F.B.I., Miss Weston," he said
politely.

She fought for some measure of composure, and all
she could stammer was a husky, shaken, "There's—s-s-s-
some mistake—my name is—Lorna Shaw."

The man stepped forward and without touching her,
seemed to force her back into the living room. She walked
backward, stumbling a little, until she brought up against
a chair and clung to it with shaking hands, her face drained
of all life and color, her eyes wide and sick, her mouth
loose-lipped.

"You've given us quite a chase, Miss Weston," said
the man softly.

"I'm—Lorna S-S-Shaw—" she stammered faintly, and
even in her own ears the words were pathetically
unconvincing.

"I don't think so, Miss Weston," said Henderson, his
voice quiet, almost polite. "We've been on your trail for
quite a while. Oh, you gave us the slip a couple of times—
I have to admit you're pretty good, Miss Weston. But of
course when Dr. Harmon testified—"

For a moment Laura felt she had received a stunning,
staggering blow, and her eyes closed, and she had to cling
to the chair hard, bend over it, fighting for breath against
that blow.

"Surprised that we found Dr. Harmon?" asked Henderson, as though puzzled that such a thing should surprise her.
"Oh, come now, Miss Weston. You are not giving us
proper credit. Naturally we looked for Dr. Harmon as soon
as we had Dr. Prescott's story. I may add that Dr. Harmon
has been most helpful."

"That—drunken witch!" Laura spat the words out in
little more than a husky whisper.

"Dr. Harmon has been discharged from the sanitarium
where you placed her—under a fictitious name and forged
papers—and has been pronounced cured," stated Henderson, still in that deceptively mild, soft voice. "And her

story tallies perfectly with Dr. Prescott's. That left us with only the necessity of finding you."

Laura pulled herself erect with a terrific effort and faced him, her head high, her eyes blazing, with a desperate last resource of something faintly approaching courage.

"I don't know what you're talking about," she stammered wildly. "I don't know any—Dr. Harmon—nor Dr. Prescott, either. The only—doctor I know is—Nick Burton —an abortionist—"

Henderson nodded, and his eyes were cold and gray.

"Yes, Mr. Burton has been helpful, too," he said quietly.

She caught her breath and her eyes were wide.

"You arrested him?" she stammered.

"I'm afraid not."

"But—why not? I tell you he's guilty—"

"He was out of our jurisdiction before his sworn affidavit reached us," said Henderson and there was a tone of regret in his voice.

"Out of—your jurisdiction?" she stammered incredulously.

"Strictly speaking, the F.B.I. has no charge against Burton," explained Henderson. "The local police have, of course—but we only come into it in cases like yours. And Burton was en route to South America, supposedly —on his honeymoon—when his affidavit was turned over to the District Attorney."

Only one word of that stuck in Laura's memory, her consciousness.

"Honeymoon?" she repeated faintly, her voice thin with incredulity.

"I understand he eloped with Marcia Courtney last night," said Henderson. "Aboard her yacht; they were married at sea by the Captain."

Laura slid down into her chair, and sat huddled like a cheap doll out of which the sawdust was spilling.

There was a vast roaring in her head; she could not hear above it. So that she did not hear footsteps moving around upstairs, and at last descending the stairs. She was unaware of the presence of the other man who came to stand in the living room doorway until he spoke to Henderson.

"No doubt about it, Chief," said the man quietly, his eyes curious upon Laura who was huddled with her face almost touching her knees, fighting down waves of nausea and faintness that threatened her. "Fingerprints match perfectly. She's Laura Weston all right."

Henderson's smile was sardonic.

"But we had no doubt of it after what Colter told us, did we?" he said almost gently, watching Laura sharply.

Slowly her head went up and her eyes upon him were sick and dazed.

"Colter?" she whispered, her voice ragged. "Colter told you I was—Laura Weston?"

"Colter told us you were fixing up an unlicensed maternity home here, and that you planned to place the babies for adoption—black market stuff. The method of it was so similar to your activities in Atlanta that we felt pretty sure you were the one we were looking for," he told her quietly. "We've been coming closer and closer to you. We'd have located you soon even if you hadn't given yourself away with that call to the D.A. For which we are very grateful, by the way. It's been quite a chase, Miss Weston—quite a chase."

Wildly, even while she knew it was hopeless, she cried out, "But I've told you and told you—I'm—not Laura Weston—"

"Look, Miss Weston," and now Henderson's voice was harsh and stern, "we have your fingerprints and you, as a nurse, should have sense enough to know that no two pair of fingerprints in the world match unless they are made by the same person! Furthermore, we have Dr. Harmon and Dr. Prescott's identification—remember this?"

He leaned down and placed a picture in her shaking hands. It was a moment before she could focus her eyes upon it; and when she could see what it was, she gave a small, stricken moan that was of utter hopeless defeat. The picture showed her sitting beside Colter, in the Tokay Club—she had not known the picture was being taken, of course. It must have been soon after she met him;

the girl-photographer had been wandering around the room; Laura had been absorbed in Colter—the flashlight bulb had not disturbed her, so many shots were being taken at nearby tables. And so she had not known that the camera had been aimed at her and Colter.

"Still want to deny that you are Laura Weston?" asked Henderson mildly.

"How—how—did you get this? And there hasn't been time for Steve and Anna to see it—" she knew she was lost but she could not go down without a fight.

"When you first mentioned to Burton what you had in mind here, he wanted no part of it—remember?" said Henderson with that oddly disturbing because so unexpected mildness, while the other man lounged in the doorway, watching her coldly, shrewdly. "Naturally, since he was under, shall we say, certain obligations to Colter, he reported to Colter what you had in mind—"

Laura's epithet for Nick was one that made even the hard-boiled man in the doorway give a small start, but Henderson went on as though Laura had not spoken.

"Colter agreed with Burton that you were riding for a fall, and because he is—well, careful of his standing in the community, he reported the matter to the D.A., who got in touch with us. Since we had been looking for you pretty anxiously, we welcomed their help," he went on. "Colter turned this picture over to the D.A., who sent it on to us. And both Dr. Harmon and Dr. Prescott identified it instantly."

"A jailbird—and a drunken dope-addict," she sneered viciously.

Henderson's eyebrows went up slightly.

"Prescott's not in jail," he told her, as though surprised. She flung up her head sharply.

"You mean they let him off?" she gasped.

"With Dr. Harmon's testimony, Dr. Prescott was completely exonerated," he told her quietly.

"And Anna?" She had realized the futility of fighting, he decided.

"Received a prison sentence, of course. Two years."

Laura's eyes flew wide with sudden hope, and a trace of color crept into her face.

"Two years," she breathed. "That's not too bad."

"With time off for good behavior, she should be out in about eighteen months—and possibly she might even do better," said Henderson, and then as though inherently he were a kindly man and did not want her to build up hope too much, he finished ominously, "But the charges against you, Miss Weston, are much more serious."

"Anna is as guilty as I am."

"It was you who arranged the adoptions, Miss Weston. We have depositions from some of the parents who are cooperating anxiously in the hope they may be allowed to keep the children you allowed them to adopt. Also, there is a charge of manslaughter in the case of the death of the woman known as 'Ann Smith.' "

"I never touched her! I had nothing to do with that!" she cried.

His eyes were cold and his voice was thin with hostility.

"Several well-established and reputable physicians testified, Miss Weston," he told her harshly. "Criminal negligence, resulting in the death of the patient, is, I believe, the charge."

She stared at him with wide, horror-stricken eyes.

Henderson studied her almost curiously.

"There are also, Miss Weston, several charges of extortion—blackmail—threatening the adoptive parents with loss of the babies unless you received certain sums," he said. He added curiously, "Funny, as smart and shrewd and cold-blooded and vicious as you have proven yourself, I'm surprised you'd write such letters. The adoptive parents furnished them to us for the prosecution. I suppose you felt it safe for you to write such letters, figuring that their fear of losing the babies would make them guard the letters from the law, or better still, burn them. . . ."

There was no longer the very tiniest atom of fight in her. She was beaten to her knees, face-down in the dust. She would go to prison like any common criminal. She would spend years and years there. She would come out, an old woman, dependent on grudging charity for her living. She had been so arrogantly sure of herself, of her cleverness, of her shrewdness, of her ability to play a dangerous game and come out the winner—and then like any damned fool little ignorant backwoods schoolgirl she had fallen for a man. Fallen so hard that she had to give herself to him. And he had taken her, laughed in her face —and thrown her into a situation so incredibly hideous that her mind was dazed trying to face it.

Henderson and the man in the doorway watched her, but neither of them was prepared for the sudden swift movement she made. She had been so defeated, so sodden in her misery that neither of them believed that she could move so purposefully. So when she came to her feet and plunged at the man in the doorway, thrusting him aside, he was caught off balance and sprawled ludicrously.

She flew up the stairs, her feet seeming scarcely to touch the treads, even while Henderson and the other man plunged after her. She reached the bathroom a step or two ahead of them, had the medicine cabinet door open and in her hand a small, fat dark brown jar of pills. As Henderson reached the door she flung back her head and jerked the whole bottle of pills into her mouth. She tried to swallow them, coughing a little, strangling a little, yet feeling some of the pills slide down her throat.

Henderson was no longer mild or gentle. He caught her by the shoulders and shook her hard, his face dark with anger.

"Oh, no, you don't, Miss Laura Weston," he told her harshly. "You're not going to run out on us that way—not while hospitals have stomach pumps and know how to use them."

She sobbed wildly as Henderson sent the car racing towards the hospital, his partner holding her in a harsh, stern grip.

THE END